TO MARRY A HIGHLAND MARAUDER

Heart of a Scot
Book Seven

By
COLLETTE CAMERON®

Blue Rose Romance®

Sweet - to - Spicy Timeless Romance®

USA Today Bestselling Author
Collette Cameron
Sweet-to-Spicy Timeless Romance®

For permission requests, write to the publisher at the address below.
Attn: Permissions Coordinator
info@collettecameronbooks.com
collettecameronbooks.com
eBook ISBN: 978-1-954307-80-3
Print Book ISBN: 978-1-966087-41-0

DEDICATION

To every reader who adores a man with a brogue.

ONE

Earl of Monteith's Ball
Edinburgh, Scotland
21 March 1721

Peeking around a Grecian column, Bethea Glanville warily scanned the illustrious assemblage. Elaborately attired, self-important gentlemen and ladies dripping in satin, velvet, every manner of jewel imaginable, and gasp-worthy towering wigs packed the breathtaking but overly-crowded ballroom.

One grand dame required two attendants, one on either side, to guide her around. Her pink ribbon-adorned white wig contained a birdcage—complete with a live and petrified-looking canary. She could scarcely move her head lest the creation either topple from her head or send her tumbling ample bosom over abundant bum.

Bethea couldn't help but wonder what would happen if the bird needed to relieve its wee self, and despite the direness of her situation, a naughty grin momentarily twitched her mouth.

Until now, she'd never considered herself a coward. She

enjoyed challenges, meeting new people, and experiencing new things. Yet the past fortnight, she'd done her utmost to avoid an amorous lord's wholly unwanted attentions.

Only now, she had begun skulking behind potted greeneries, diving into curtained alcoves, and made so many excuses to seek the lady's retiring room that people might've begun pondering if a health condition plagued her.

Odin's gnarly teeth. How had she ever thought *this* was what she wanted?

How many times had she and her sister, Branwen, complained to their guardian, Keane Buchannan, Duke of Roxdale, that he was too strict and protective? That they longed to attend elaborate fetes and soirees such as this very ball? That at one and twenty, she was of marriageable age, and she wanted to fall in love, marry, and have children?

Well, not precisely this minute or week or month even, but in due course.

In truth, Bethea thoroughly enjoyed the dancing and the gaiety. The musical performances, teas, and all the rest were exhausting but exciting, nonetheless. Though she wasn't the belle of any ball, enough gentlemen had asked her to dance and otherwise paid her pretty compliments that she had a grand time thus far.

When noxious David Talbot, Earl of Monteith, wasn't following her and sniffing about her skirts, that was. Rarely— never before, in truth— had she met anyone as off-putting and as persistent as the earl. He was worse than a ratty terrier after a meaty bone.

Pursing her mouth at the thought, Bethea stood on her tiptoes, craning her neck to see over the milling merrymakers and dancers. Tonight's assembled were some of the most extravagant she'd seen, and she couldn't help but be slightly impressed at the earl's scope of influence—even if she intensely disliked the man himself.

Where are they?

She gripped the column tighter, scrutinizing the undulating crowd which seemed to have swallowed her sister, Keane, and his lovely new wife, Marjorie.

Wait. Squinting, Bethea arched even higher on her toes. *Is that...?* For an elated instant, she hoped she'd spotted a familiar raven head, shoulders above the milling assemblage.

Was Camden Kennedy here?

The notion caused a little thrill of excitement to rush through her, immediately followed by her knitting her eyebrows together into a perplexed vee.

Odd, but neither Keane nor Marjorie had mentioned that Camden—one of her first husband's brothers—was even in Edinburgh, let alone expected here tonight.

In a blink, the throng shifted, obstructing whoever the man was from her avid view. Inexplicable disappointment swept Bethea. She'd very much wanted him to be Camden Kennedy.

Standing well over six feet, all brawn and muscle, but with a perpetual twinkle in his vivid blue eyes, Camden would've kept her safe from Monteith. Now *there* was a man she could trust not to impose himself on her. Not once in the times that she'd encountered Camden had he stepped beyond the mark in word or action.

A practiced flirt possessing a disarming wit, he usually made her laugh too.

A heavy-treaded, unsteady *clickety-clop, clickety-clop* announced the Earl of Monteith's approach before she smelled the perpetually malodorous man.

Lovely.

Daring another peek, she stifled a distressed gasp.

Drat, drat, and double drat-damn.

The very man she'd managed to avoid the past hour toddled toward her on absurdly embellished blue and silver high-heeled shoes, perspiration profusely beading the wide expanse of his brow and upper lip. His ridiculously curled wig brushed his shoulders, and she strongly suspected a number of vermin made the wig their home. The engraved, shiny silver buttons fastened across his stomach strained to contain his corpulence.

By all the saints, if he sneezed, the fastenings would become lethal projectiles.

Her mouth quivered again at the image of the prestigious guests in attendance laid out flat by flying buttons.

Her mirth, however, was short-lived.

The Earl of Monteith, and her host for this evening, had found her. *Again.* The nobleman was persistent, if nothing else. No amount of politely discouraging the middling-aged man's attentions deterred him from his pointed pursuit of her since her family had arrived in Edinburgh.

Tattle had it, he was in the market for a countess, and apparently, he'd set his bleary, dumpling-eyed sights on her. Bethea had done nothing to encourage his interest, and the more she attempted to put him off, the more determined he had become to seek her out. Like a great perspiring and smelly hound on the scent.

If he hadn't already, she truly feared Monteith meant to ask Keane for her hand.

God save her from such a horrific fate.

A shudder rippled up her spine, spreading out in prickly waves across her shoulders and tingling her scalp. The very notion made the small midday meal she'd consumed threaten to reappear.

Swallowing, Bethea pressed a hand to her middle, willing the queasiness roiling there to abate.

Keane wouldn't betroth her without telling her.

She had no doubt of that, and Marjorie well knew Bethea and Branwen desired a love-match. A widowed Englishwoman, Marjorie had become the older sister Bethea had never had, and both she and Branwen had confided their dreams and fears to her.

A curious, rather austere lady caught her peeping around the column, and Bethea couldn't resist a mischievous little finger wave. When the woman promptly elevated her reedy nose and turned her back in a direct snub, Bethea chuckled. Only since arriving in Edinburgh and experiencing the—ah—*flamboyant* and—ah—*interesting* persons of elevated station had this peculiar bend toward precociousness overcome her.

Standing on her toes again, Bethea desperately searched the room for Branwen, Keane, or Marjorie. She didn't know anyone else well enough to approach them. *If only that had been Camden Kennedy.* In truth, she shouldn't be hiding here alone. There were those only too eager to cast aspersions on something as innocent as an unchaperoned lass.

And I was so eager to experience High Society.

Bethea huffed a rude noise beneath her breath, not daring to voice the unladylike oath she wasn't even supposed to know, let alone utter.

Bent on a hasty retreat, she gathered the iridescent silver and lavender of her satin gown in her gloved hands. She might very well heave decorum aside and cause a scandal by hiking her skirts to her knees and sprinting across the room. Anything to avoid Monteith.

How she wished she was back at Trentwick Castle in the Highlands right now. Boredom was, indeed, preferable to hiding at every event and dreading an unwanted proposal.

She cast another desperate glance about the ballroom.

Praise the heavens.

There Marjorie was. Her fiery red tresses were a much welcome, glowing beacon.

"Miss Glanville," the earl puffed breathlessly from several paces away.

Och, hell in a basket.

Determined to avoid a dance as unpleasant as the one she'd suffered through at the Cavendishs' two nights ago, Bethea pretended not to hear him. His fetid scent had compelled her to hold her breath each time the reel's steps forced them together. Without glancing behind her, she dove into the throng, winding her way through the guests.

Several people smiled or inclined their heads—two or three gentlemen quite lecherously—but mindful of Marjorie's instruction, Bethea maintained an air of genial indifference as she swiftly wove through the colorful tapestry of people. The instinct to run, to put as much distance as possible between herself and the Earl of Monteith, thrummed through her.

Nevertheless, she kept her pace brisk yet modulated.

"At all times, present yourselves as polite and approachable, but not eager or forward," Marjorie had counseled her and Branwen when Keane had, at last, conceded to present them in Edinburgh. "A young lady must act agreeable without seeming overly-friendly toward any gentlemen. A very fine line exists between politesse and what some consider fast or impudent behavior," Marjorie had solemnly advised.

No doubt, naughtily waving at a busybody fell into the latter category.

So many ridiculous rules to observe, half of which, Marjorie and Keane dolefully acknowledged, changed on a whim.

Be reserved, but not austere.

Smile, but not coyly.

Exemplify graciousness, but do not encourage or tolerate scandalous behavior.

And on and on and *on* went the list of strictures and expectations. How could anyone possibly be themselves?

No wonder Keane hadn't been enthusiastic about toting them to Edinburgh and enduring the social scene. A constant, unnerving undercurrent hummed beneath the outward facades of geniality, and Bethea had already learned not to take anyone at their word.

Pulse high and breathing erratic from the discomfiture the Earl of Monteith always roused, Bethea tried not to draw undue attention as she slowed her steps to a sedate pace and approached Marjorie.

Attired in a stunning sea-green gown that set off her bronze hair to perfection, she chatted with a trio of attractive ladies. Marjorie spied her, and producing a welcoming smile, she extended her hand and drew Bethea near her. Her treacle-brown gaze gravitated past Bethea, and flexing the merest bit, comprehension dawned in the depths of her eyes.

Perfect. Just as Bethea had hoped.

Aye, Keane had made a brilliant choice in selecting this exceptional woman for his duchess. Not only was she warm and loving, but her two adorable daughters had brought much laughter to the keep.

"Your sister is dancing at the moment," Marjorie said in her lilting English accent, one eye trained on Monteith's laborious progress. "And Keane excused himself a few minutes ago and left the ballroom with Mr. Frederick Rickerson and the Marquis of Pennsworth." Jollity shone in her eyes. "They claimed they had important *business* to discuss."

One of the other women, a petite brunette with a shy smile, chuckled and arched an eyebrow. Lady Abagail

Fitzpatrick, if Bethea recalled correctly. "Which means they stole off to have a stiff drink. No doubt to congratulate Roxdale for having the good sense to marry you, Your Grace."

Before Marjorie had a chance to introduce Bethea to the other pair, Monteith was upon them. Except for Marjorie, the ladies dipped into perfunctory curtsies, though she angled her head. She outranked him but nonetheless curved her mouth into a gracious smile. Her nose only twitched the merest bit as his overpowering stench wafted near.

Bethea wouldn't even permit her imagination to conjure up an image of what bedding him would entail. *You needn't fear on that account,* she reminded herself. Keane would never consent to such a match.

Would he?

She bit her lower lip, traitorous uncertainty pricking her.

He was most determined to improve the duchy's standing and reputation, and if one of his wards were to marry a powerful earl...

Nae. I shallna think of it.

Lady Fitzpatrick promptly snapped her fan open and went about creating a vigorous breeze as the other two women surreptitiously stepped backward a few paces. It said much about Monteith's sphere of influence that so many guests graced his ballroom, despite his hygiene issue.

Did Monteith truly have no knowledge of how offensive his body odor was?

Perhaps he had an unfortunate condition that caused the malodorousness.

Why else would he not address the embarrassing matter?

"Yer Grace, might I call upon ye and His Grace tomorrow afternoon?" Monteith half-wheezed, sending Bethea a sly look from beneath his heavily hooded gaze. His smile crinkled the fleshy, wrinkled pouches drooping beneath his eyes. "I have a matter of some import I wish to discuss with him. A matter I'm confident he'll be amenable to."

Good God! Nae.

Bethea's heart stopped beating before plummeting straight to her lavender silk shoes. Her throat went dry as hot sand, and an icy chill swamped her.

It was just as she'd feared.

He intended to ask Keane for her hand in marriage.

Marjorie still held her hand, and Bethea squeezed hard, sending a silent, panicked message.

Monteith had some nerve cornering Marjorie when others were present, thereby making the refusal of his request more awkward. The boor should've sent a card around requesting an audience. However, Bethea had learned another thing about Monteith: no one's opinion of him exceeded his own.

Please say nae. Please say nae, she mentally chanted, hoping her eyes didn't reveal her absolute desperation. The fact that every ounce of blood in her body had drained to her toes wouldn't give her away either.

"I regret we shan't be home tomorrow," Marjorie said coolly with the perfect combination of solicitousness and inflexibility. And praise the saints, she didn't offer an explanation as to where they would be, for the earl was brazen enough to put in an appearance.

Thank God.

Marjorie serenely scanned the ballroom before returning her attention to him. "I see this set has ended, my lord, and my husband's other ward is searching for us. I take my role as chaperone very seriously and must make my way to her, your lordship. Please excuse us."

A tinge of steel threaded her last words.

With a cordial nod to the ladies, each of their expressions

schooled into blandness but a knowing glint in their eyes, she led Bethea away.

"Has he been pestering you, Bethea?" Marjorie asked beneath her breath as they fell into step, putting several feet between themselves and the pungent earl.

"Aye, and I can scarcely relax and enjoy myself. I've taken to hidin' or lurkin' in shadows. Monteith makes my skin crawl." Bethea extracted her hand and then fitted it into Marjorie's bent arm. "I fear he means to propose, and I canna abide him, Marjorie." A note of anxiousness crept into her voice. "Keane wouldna—"

"Lord have mercy, no." Marjorie gave a vigorous shake of her head. "Never think it, my dear. He thinks Monteith's a sweaty toad, but the earl does have valuable connections. We'll need to put Monteith off without offending him. I've already extracted a promise from Keane that you and Branwen will have your choice of husbands."

"Have I told ye how glad I am Keane married ye?" Bethea pressed nearer to Marjorie's side, a wide grin arcing her mouth. "I didna ken how we managed without ye before."

Marjorie squeezed her arm. "And I'm delighted he has wards who could be the younger sisters I never had."

They were upon Branwen now, resplendent in midnight blue and white. Her stance uneven, she offered a pained smile. "I fear my last partner trod upon my feet so many times that my toes are severely bruised. I believe I'll rest for a few minutes in the ladies' retirin' room. Hopefully, puttin' my feet up will do the trick."

"I'll go with ye," Bethea offered, seizing the excuse to help her sister and avoid Monteith.

Marjorie nodded. "I'll let Keane know."

"Ah, there you are, Marjorie." A pretty, plump woman with light brown hair and a radiant smile approached. "I've been searching for you all evening." Her curious gaze gravitated to Bethea and her sister. "And these must be Keane's wards."

"Anna, I didn't know you were in Scotland." Marjorie bussed her cheek. "Yes, this is Bethea." She indicated Bethea with a sweep of her hand. "And Branwen Glanville. Girls, this is Anna Buchannan Hawthorne. She's actually a second or third cousin to Keane. We were girlhood friends."

Anna laughed, a merry twinkle in her pale brown eyes. "Well, my branch of the family rarely ventured north of the border, and that's why I've never met you in all this time."

"'Tis a pleasure," Bethea greeted. "How wonderful that ye were friends, and now ye're cousins."

"Indeed," Branwen agreed, shifting on her feet and grimacing slightly.

She truly was uncomfortable.

Marjorie linked her elbow with Anna's. "The girls were just on their way to the retiring room, but why don't we find a quiet corner and catch up?"

"A splendid idea," Anna agreed. "Ten years is far too long."

"I'll come for you in half an hour," Marjorie told Bethea and Branwen before turning away, her coppery head bent to hear what Anna was saying.

Bethea promptly wrapped an arm around Branwen's waist and slowly guided her slightly taller sister from the ballroom. Though Branwen put on a brave face, her pinched lips and occasional flinches revealed the state of her damaged feet.

Ladies ought to be warned of Lord Hurstwood's proclivity to mash his partners' feet.

"Ye poor darlin'," Bethea murmured as they entered the corridor.

"Lord Hurstwood is an exuberant dance partner, and I

vow he tromped upon my toes a score of times." Branwen winced again, and a small gasp escaped her.

Lord Hurstwood was no small man either. Not given to corpulence like Monteith, Hurstwood was nonetheless a thick, stocky sort an inch or two over six feet.

Alarm spiked in Bethea.

Just how badly injured were Branwen's feet?

Bethea's scalp tingled, and she had the unmistakable sensation that someone watched her. As she turned the corner, she cut a swift glance along the passage. Her flesh puckered when she spotted the Earl of Monteith, his bulbous form framed in the ballroom's entrance, staring at her with unfettered lust upon his fleshy face.

A sly smile curved his full mouth, and he boldly winked.

Just as she jerked her focus away, Camden Kennedy's massive form appeared behind the earl. He looked straight at her, and a scintillating current sparked between them.

He is *here.*

When had he arrived?

And more mystifying, why hadn't he sought her family out?

TWO

Clenching his teeth, Camden speared a darkling glower at the Earl of Monteith's broad, fleshy back. He'd seen the devil's spawn ogling Bethea from across the ballroom, and when the earl had followed her and Branwen, Camden had momentarily set aside his purpose for being here tonight.

The instinct to shield Bethea from the lecherous tosspot thrummed through him, echoing with each strident step he took across the crowded room. His need to protect Bethea proved a dangerous distraction.

One he couldn't afford at the moment, damn it all.

In truth, he hadn't intended to attend tonight's ball, and he hadn't informed Marjorie or Keane of his last-minute change in plans. As the widow of their older brother Sion, Camden and his brother Graeme still considered Marjorie their sister.

They always would.

The death of a family member didn't negate the relationship forged over the years.

Keane was his cousin, although there'd been little interaction between the two branches of the family for almost three decades. However, the Buchannans and Kennedys had reconciled their differences, and Camden had come to like and respect his ducal, sometimes stodgy, cousin.

He liked Keane's eldest ward even more, although he'd not permitted himself to contemplate why. His was a dangerous life, running covert operations for the Crown, and although he enjoyed a lush, feminine body warming his bed, he wasn't ready to take a bride. Doing so assuredly meant relinquishing his role as an agent.

Dragging in a steadying breath, and reminding himself of the importance of his

mission—and that bloodying the nose of his host wouldn't help advance that purpose—he shifted his focus beyond Monteith.

Camden met Bethea's startled gaze across the distance. Her beautiful silver-gray eyes went round as the moon, and her delicate raven eyebrows arched high on her forehead.

A glint of welcome shone in her avid gaze, but a stark question did as well.

Why didna ye tell anyone ye'd be here tonight?

In truth, he'd hoped to avoid his cousin, Marjorie, and the Glanville sisters in this throng, along with revealing the details required to explain his presence in Edinburgh. He'd meant to locate tonight's target and furtively observe Sir Phillip Etherington until the Englishman slunk away for his clandestine meeting that was supposed to occur during the ball.

Then Camden, Bryston McPherson, and their men would follow the scunner, apprehend him en route to meet his contact, and relieve him of the incriminating evidence His Majesty sought.

There were far too many things that could go wrong with that plan. Nonetheless, Etherington had indeed arrived almost an hour ago and, as was his wont, had scarcely spoken to anyone, let alone danced. He was, quite obviously, as uncomfortable and out of place as a strumpet in a convent.

Bethea's attention flickered to Monteith for an instant, and genuine fear shadowed her refined features.

The earl terrified her, Camden realized with an unpleasant start that ignited a spark of fury.

If Monteith had said or done anything...

Nae, he swiftly reassured himself.

Keane was most protective of his wards. Monteith wouldn't dare go beyond the bounds of propriety, or he'd risk Keane's wrath. Monteith might be a powerful earl, but Keane was the Duke of Roxdale. A near legend in Scotland, and only an imbecile dismissed him offhandedly.

And yet, Monteith openly leered at her.

Well, that wasn't precisely true.

Camden brushed a hand over his jaw as he eyed the earl, still avidly peering down the corridor.

The earl had let his guard down when he wasn't aware others observed him, and with his back to the guests, only Bethea and her sister could see his face. Branwen appeared to be in some distress. Leaning heavily on Bethea, she kept her gaze trained upon the floor.

Branwen murmured something, and pulling her gaze from Camden, Bethea bent her sable head near her sister's slightly darker head as she guided the taller girl into the room. The door shut firmly behind them.

From what Camden's informant had briefly told him about the house's layout, that chamber was the retiring room, and Monteith wouldn't dare intrude upon the ladies' hallowed ground.

Or would he?

What did Camden know of Monteith, other than that he was wealthy, powerful, and a sycophant always toadying for the king's attention? Oh, and he had an eye for young ladies and a penchant for whoring. In all likelihood, the man probably had the clap.

Time to ponder and investigate that later, and by God, Camden would.

Right now, he needed to return his attention to the reason he was here tonight. Putting his thoughts of Bethea and Monteith aside, he faced the ballroom and sought Bryston McPherson, also a covert agent for the Crown.

Several ladies gave the ominous-looking Scot with a thin scar lashing his left cheek wary glances and a wide berth. As was his habit, Bryston had pulled his long blond hair back on the sides and secured it in a knot at the back of his head. His size and features revealed his Norse heritage.

Neither Camden nor Bryston had any particular love for King George I, but they did for Scotland. There were those only too happy to drag Scotland into another brutal war. More violence, more killing and death, more sorrow and heartache.

The King had quashed two uprisings in the last few years, but Camden feared there would always be Scots resistant to English rule. He didn't blame them, and in truth, understood their frustration. But by damn, Scotland and her people had suffered enough.

A wound never healed if constantly picked. Scotland was very much like that.

Bryston jutted his strong chin toward the terrace, and Camden gave an infinitesimal nod indicating he understood. Casually strolling the ballroom's perimeter, he avoided looking directly at anyone as he made his way to the exit.

Disguised as highwaymen, six men awaited him in an alley a half street away.

Unlike Camden and Bryston, these Scots hadn't been

retained for clandestine operations at His Majesty's behest. Fearless, ferocious fighters, and utterly ruthless, the mercenaries awaiting him and Bryston fought for whatever man possessed the heaviest purse.

And because Camden acted as an extension of His Majesty, that man was him. For now.

In truth, his superior, Sir Walter Makepeace, had brought these mercenaries on board, adamant that the nature of this assignment called for men of a different ilk than trained agents or soldiers.

It still struck Camden as irregular that in all the missions he'd participated in, only this one, led by Makepeace, required hired mercenaries.

Camden wholeheartedly disagreed with Makepeace's assessment, but wary and watchful, he followed orders nevertheless.

Tonight marked the eighth time they'd detained a coach in an attempt to catch the traitor.

Every other time, Etherington had eluded them, which was why they'd changed tactics and opted to watch the Englishman's every move tonight. He'd sent out a decoy coach as usual, but this time, Camden was ready for his trickery.

His position with the Crown had required him to take on the persona of a smuggler and marauder. Bryston, on the other hand, had truly sailed the seas for nigh on a decade as a buccaneer. Captain of his own ship, he'd carried letters of marque sanctifying his privateering.

An intimidating man, he boasted several piercings and tattoos. When he'd left his former life, he agreed to join Camden as an agent for His Majesty, not quite ready to relinquish an adventurer's life just yet.

To this day, Camden didn't know what caused Bryston to

leave the life of a seafarer abruptly, and he hadn't asked. Some things a man didn't share.

"Shall we be about it, then?" Camden said as he fell into step beside Bryston.

"Aye," Bryston agreed with a terse nod. Lowering his voice as they approached the footmen standing at attention, he murmured, "I have men watchin' every exit. They'll give the signal the second that English turd pokes his beak out."

Boot heels clacking on the charcoal gray and white tiled marble foyer, they strode toward the door. For the benefit of the crimson and gold liveried footmen standing at attention on either side of the entrance, as well anyone else watching, Camden slapped Bryston heartily upon the back. "What say ye we find ourselves a bit of *real* entertainment?" he said loudly.

"Aye," Bryston chuckled and jeered. "I canna watch any more of those foplin's and coxcombs prancin' about like banty roosters." One pinky in the air and his mouth pursed, he demonstrated a few mincing steps.

The corner of a footman's mouth twitched as if he agreed with Bryston's assessment.

Oh, to be able to see inside the mind of a servant. What tales they might tell.

Moments later, he and Bryston tripped down the immaculate front stairs. The dank, damp air encircled them as they sauntered down the cobbled lane. Camden casually glanced over his shoulder before giving a slight nod, and they slipped into the side street.

It only took a few moments to divest himself of his evening jacket and exchange it for a black, wool coat to match those of his comrades. Wrapping a black scarf around his neck, he nodded to Bryston.

"Ye take three men and find a place to conceal yerselves

along Wester Road. The others will ride with me, and we'll do the same on Easter Road."

They must catch Etherington before he boarded the ship at Leith, and aside from Leith Walk, those were the two main routes between Edinburgh and Leith.

Camden disregarded Leith Walk as an escape route for Etherington. The Englishman enjoyed his creature comforts too much. He wouldn't trudge two miles on foot to the port in the fog and drizzle this time of night.

No, he'd take Easter or Wester Roads, and Camden would place his money on Easter.

He crammed a knitted cap upon his head, as did Bryston before tugging on black leather gloves. Except for their mounts and varying sizes, the men were indistinguishable from one another.

Exactly as Camden had planned.

A handful of minutes later, the men mounted, and he straightened in the saddle, taking in each hireling one by one. "Nae matter who snares Etherin'ton, we'll meet nae later than four in the mornin'."

Only he and Bryston knew the particular location of that rendezvous, The Boar and Brew—an unobtrusive inn outside Dalkeith. From there, they'd transport Etherington to England to meet whatever fate His Majesty deemed appropriate.

Much would depend on the evidence Etherington carried on him tonight and how cooperative he proved during his interrogation. In all likelihood, no matter how forthcoming he was, he'd swing from the gallows for his treachery.

And, if all went as anticipated, this plotting to overthrow the king would cease. For the sake of Scotland and her people, it must. Scotland needed to heal, and constant turmoil and insurrection prevented that. If the time ever came for Scotland to regain her independence from England again—*peacefully*—Camden would be the first to celebrate.

Hunched down and slightly slumped, giving the appearance of a pished tippler slowly making his way home, Camden reigned his mount out of the wynd first.

As arranged, his men gradually followed, keeping their distance from one another so as not to raise suspicion. The ring of the horses' hooves echoing on the slick cobblestones penetrated the night.

Occasionally, necks bent and collars raised against the cool breeze, men scurried by. A skinny dog slunk past, its tail between his legs, and cats yowled angrily in the distance as they did before a fight commenced.

Over the past fifteen minutes, the drizzle had transformed into large raindrops, and the fog had thickened until he could only see a few feet ahead.

Camden went over the ambush several times in his head until he was positive he'd considered every possibility. After Etherington's capture, they'd seek his conspirator.

Several of Monteith's guests tonight were known to harbor less than loyal sentiments toward the king. Not that George I had earned the Scots' or, for that matter, the English's respect and admiration.

Satisfied with the evening's progress so far, at least as far as snaring the traitor to the Crown, he allowed his mind to wander to Bethea.

Thinking about her definitely didn't bring the same degree of gratification.

Bethea's pale face as she'd stood in the corridor, an arm wrapped around her sister's waist, lurched to the forefront of his mind. Wearing an exquisite lavender and silver gown, the toes of her lavender silk shoes peeking out from beneath the hem, her beauty had staggered him like a punch to the gut.

Once more, he recalled the graceful slant of her jaw and cheeks, the elegant arch of her creamy neck, and the glossy sheen of her ebony upswept hair.

He scratched his jaw, trying to recall just how long the Glanville sisters had been Roxdale's wards.

Fifteen years?

Aye, that seemed about right.

Most of Bethea's and Branwen's lives then. Point of fact, they were more like Keane's adopted sisters than his wards, and therefore, essentially cousins to the Kennedys as well.

That must be what stirred his protective instincts—the familial connection. Monteith had threatened his kin and even now was a threat to Bethea.

Camden sensed it with every nerve, pore, and fiber of his being.

Aye, but gazing upon female kin had never heated his blood or caused blood to rush to his loins before.

THREE

Even as Bethea helped her sister to one of the turquoise and gold brocade couches, Camden's fierce expression intruded upon her thoughts. He'd looked ready to pummel Monteith.

On her behalf?

It rather thrilled her to think so.

With a hitch in her breathing and a grimace contorting her pretty face, Branwen gingerly sank onto the cushions. "I vow, I'm done for the night."

"Darlin', why ever did ye continue dancin' with him if he was stompin' upon yer toes?" Bethea asked sympathetically.

"I felt sorry for him." Branwen summoned a wry smile and putting a hand to her forehead, shut her eyes. "He's rather nice, but clumsy as an ox in the proverbial china shop."

So like Branwen. Her compassionate nature made her vulnerable.

"I overheard several ladies refuse him," she said. "Some quite ruthlessly, I might add. When Lord Hurstwood approached me, he looked so hopeful, and I didna have the heart to say nae. Now I ken why they were reluctant to accept his offer to dance."

Bethea shook her head, a small empathetic smile tugging at her lips. "Honestly, I'm no' sure whether to be outraged or amused. I confess, I pity the poor man, but surely he must be aware of his deficit."

Cracking an eyelid open, her sister arched a midnight brow. She gave a dubious shake of her head. "Trust me. He is no'. I both admire his oblivion and am confounded by it."

"Well, I assure ye, should he ask me, I shall have to decline." Bethea knelt before her sister and cautiously removed her shoes. "I have nae wish to have my toes mashed. I shall suggest a sedate walk about the ballroom, or if the weather permits, upon the veranda."

Branwen inhaled sharply and clamped her teeth upon her lower lip as Bethea freed her sister's foot.

"Forgive me, dearest," she apologized, hating that she'd hurt her sister. But the shoes must come off so that she could see the damage and determine the best course of action. "I am tryin' to be gentle."

"I ken." Her face strained, Branwen let her eyelash flutter shut again. "I confess, I'm afraid to look."

The second shoe followed the first. Thankfully, no blood marred the fine silk stockings.

"Ye just relax, and I'll look for both of us," Bethea assured her, not certain she wanted to see her sister's abused feet either.

Taking care not to jostle or bump Branwen's feet more than necessary, she rolled her sister's stockings down. She slipped the first shoe off and couldn't suppress her gasp. Bruises had already begun to form on her sister's reddened toes and even atop her feet.

"That bad?" Branwen whispered, keeping her eyelids firmly shut.

Bethea chose her words with care. "Yer nae bleedin', but ye're no' goin' to be able to walk for several days, I fear."

A tiny part of Bethea rejoiced because, now, she'd have a legitimate excuse to stay home and avoid another encounter with the wretched Earl of Monteith. *But also miss opportunities to find a potential husband,* her annoying conscience quipped.

Balderdash.

She hadn't come to Edinburgh with the express purpose of finding a husband. That would merely be an added benefit. *Mayhap.* Bethea wasn't so desperate to get married that she'd marry without love.

After removing the second stocking, she pushed to her feet. "Let's put a cool cloth on them. That should help with the swellin'."

"Ye dinna think the damage is worse than it looks?" Branwen raised her legs a couple of inches, and a frown knitted her forehead. She angled her abused feet back and forth.

Hopefully, no'.

Bethea shook her head. "Nae. I dinna think there are any broken bones. Yer shoes protected ye from that."

She crossed to an ewer and basin, beside which lay a stack of neatly folded linens. After removing her gloves, she poured a measure of water into the basin, then saturated two cloths. Once she'd wrung them out, she returned to Branwen, now resting her head against the back of the sofa.

"I shall inform Marjorie or Keane that we must depart at once." Draping the cool, damp squares over her sister's damaged feet, she glanced upward. "Ye canna possibly leave through the main doors, unless someone carries ye."

It wouldn't be Keane.

He'd broken his wrist in January and was still recovering his strength.

Branwen vigorously shook her head. "Nae, there must be

another way. I dinna want more unkind things said about Lord Hurstwood, and I have nae desire to be the object of the rumormongers' attention."

Of course, she'd consider Lord Hurstwood's feelings.

A faint frown drew her fine eyebrows together. "There are *vipers* out there." She canted her head toward the closed door. "Marjorie warned us about their cruelty, but I didna understand just how nasty people can be."

She was absolutely right.

Through those elaborate panels mingled pretentious popinjays, and painted and perfumed ladies whose shrewd-eyed gazes lit with excitement at the merest hint of scandal, impropriety, or gossip. They thrived on others' mistakes and calamities as if misfortune somehow elevated their standing.

"I'll see if there's an inconspicuous way to depart," Bethea said.

Surely a house this size must have a dozen exterior exits. Bethea considered the door on the other side of the room and angled her head in that direction.

"Perhaps through there." She pointed at the door on the other side of the room. "I believe there's a terrace or veranda on this side of the house."

Earlier, she'd seen a porch of some sort through the tall glass doors on one end of the ballroom.

Her sister gave an unconvinced nod and puffed out her cheeks. "And I was so eager to experience High Society."

As had Bethea been.

Branwen chuckled dryly and cocked an eyebrow in skepticism. "I must confess to havin' regrets."

"I had similar thoughts myself not even fifteen minutes ago," Bethea admitted. "As I was dodgin' the Earl of Monteith again."

Screwing her mouth in distaste, Branwen said, "He really has become an obnoxious pest, hasna he?"

"Aye, and he asked Marjorie if he could call tomorrow." Hugging herself, Bethea rubbed her hands up and down her bare arms. "He's goin' to ask for my hand. I ken he is. But, thank God, Marjorie has persuaded Keane that we should be allowed to choose our husbands."

"She is a dear, and I'm verra glad Keane married her," Branwen said, settling further back onto the couch.

"As am I," Bethea agreed.

They'd taken to Marjorie, and she to them, as if they'd known each other their entire lives.

Bethea leaned down and bussed a kiss across her sister's soft cheek. "I'll be back in a few minutes with Marjorie and Keane, and we'll get ye home and settled comfortably. I think it would be wise to have a physician examine yer feet too."

"Nae." Branwen shook her head. "Let's see how I am tomorrow. I truly believe my feet and toes are merely bruised." She grinned and waggled her winged black eyebrows mischievously. "Just think. We have an excuse to stay in, read before the fire, or play games."

"Good heavens! Is this the same sister who lamented we'd end up whiskery-chinned old tabbies with a collection of purrin' cats durin' the Hogmanay celebration?" Bethea teased as she crossed to the other door.

Her sentiments exactly matched Branwen's.

Perhaps the quieter, more sedate life of the Highlands wasn't so very disagreeable after all. An unexpected pang of homesickness fluttered behind her ribs, like a caged sparrow trying to escape.

Uncertain what she'd find on the other side, Bethea turned the key in the lock, and then tentatively lowered the handle and drew the panel open a couple of inches. Head cocked, she listened, and upon hearing nothing, boldly pulled the door wide, exposing what appeared to be an antechamber.

It was dark, except for the faint illumination filtering in from a single, tall terrace window and a wedge of light streaming in from another partially ajar door on the room's far side.

Angling back to her sister, she gave a jaunty little wave. "I'll return shortly. Dinna do anythin' I wouldna do," she quipped, gratified to hear Branwen laugh at the jest.

With that, Bethea slipped through the opening, closing the door behind her. Treading softly upon the thick carpet, lest someone occupy the other room, she considered the burning question that had plagued her these past ten minutes or so.

Why hadn't Camden made his presence known to them this evening?

And why had he looked like he'd like to tear the Earl of Monteith limb from limb?

She'd never seen Camden angry before, but the severe slash of his dark eyebrows, the granite-like contours of his face, and unyielding line of his mouth left no doubt he'd been fuming. Flames had flashed in his blue eyes, and didn't blue fire always burn the hottest?

She supposed she'd have to ask him what had his hackles up when next she saw him.

Once at the opposite door, she peeked around the door-frame, unwilling to interrupt a *tête-à-tête* or a clandestine assignation. Marjorie had warned her, quite severely, in fact, that dalliances of that nature were not uncommon at social gatherings or court. Bethea must use every caution not to be caught alone with a gentleman, no matter how innocuous on her part.

To do so spelled certain ruin.

A relieved sigh filtered past her parted lips at finding the chamber empty.

Candles glowed in brass and umber marble sconces on either side of the elaborate beveled mirrored mantelpiece. Bookshelves of the same lustrous dark wood flanked the fireplace. Behind an intricate screen, a fire crackled merrily, and yet, for all of the room's grandeur, it lacked cheer and warmth.

A study or office, she presumed.

The aroma of ink, paper, burning wood, and cigars clung to the furnishings and draperies. Catching a lingering whiff of the sickly-sweet smell that surrounded Monteith, she wrinkled her nose.

A double door led onto the terrace, which paralleled the side of the house. Just as she'd thought. A perfect way to unobtrusively bundle Branwen to the coach. Perhaps Camden could be imposed upon to carry her since Keane shouldn't. She'd request a footman locate Camden while she informed Keane and Marjorie of Branwen's condition.

The evening was cool and damp, and a swift glance out the window confirmed Bethea's suspicion. No guests made use of the terrace or gardens. Besides, it had rained all day, and even now, the steady *drip, drip, drip* of rainwater from the eaves confirmed the outdoors was inhospitable to even the most robust guests.

As she skirted two wingback leather chairs positioned beside a tall table bearing a cigar stub in an ashtray, the *snick* of the door handle launched her heart to her throat, and her heartbeat accelerated.

Someone meant to enter.

FOUR

Though Bethea wasn't doing anything wrong, alarm pumped through her, nevertheless. She could explain her presence. However, she conceded, even her presence might appear suspicious to someone with a distrustful mind.

Should she stand her ground and clarify that she merely searched for another exit from the house because of Branwen's ill-used toes? Or should she retreat?

God and all the saints, what if it was Monteith on the other side of the door?

In all probability, it was, and she wasn't about to be alone with the man. He might take liberties that would compel her to accept his hand.

Never, she silently vowed.

Never would she enter into a forced or arranged marriage, or a marriage of convenience. Better to remain unwed than subject herself to a lifetime with a man she didn't love. Or, in Monteith's case, a man she couldn't abide.

That thought sent her fleeing, and she'd just dashed around the corner of the adjacent chamber, yanking her skirts inside, when the door whisked open. She pressed into the corner behind the door. Her heart hammering against her ribcage, she covered her quivering mouth with one hand and pressed her fluttering stomach hard with the other.

That had been much, *much* too close.

"You were able to convince them to swear their allegiance? In writing?" A man asked in a haughty, English accent, his voice grating like broken pieces of china grinding together.

She gathered her skirts closer and caught the inside of her lower lip between her teeth. Her heart thumped so loudly in her ears that she was certain the men could hear its erratic pounding. Leaning forward a couple of inches, she squinted through the crack between the door and the doorframe.

A tall, cadaverous man with waxy, jaundiced skin and a prominent, hooked nose stood indolently, a bony knee bent and an even bonier hand on his hip. He wore stark black from his wig to his plain shoes, which made the frothy white lace at his throat and the large ruby ring on his forefinger oddly discordant with the rest of his severe appearance.

She didn't recognize him, nor had she seen him amongst the guests tonight. Though, she reminded herself, she hadn't seen Camden either, until he'd appeared like an avenging marauder behind Monteith.

Her breath caught, almost choking her, as Monteith wandered across her line of vision.

Good God. I'd rather face down a charging rhino or a starving lion than encounter him.

She clapped a hand over her mouth again, lest she give herself away.

The crow-like man roved his bored gaze languidly around the chamber, and her skin prickled at the complete lack of emotion in his too-close, wintery gray eyes.

Who was he?

Were those pockmarks covering his skeletal features?

His lips thinned further, reminding her of a serpent.

Without a doubt, he was the most unnerving man Bethea had ever beheld. Even worse, impossible as it seemed, than Monteith.

Removing her hand from her mouth, she darted a frantic glance at the closed door a few feet away. She'd retreat into the ladies' retiring room but feared discovery. She'd done nothing wrong, yet guilt assailed her. Or perhaps it was a premonition that these two men couldn't be up to any good, slithering away during a ball.

Never had time crept along so slowly.

"Well, Monteith?" snapped the Englishman, impatiently tapping his thigh with his fingertips. "Did you, or didn't you? Has tonight been another waste of my time? Just like all the others? In truth, I'm beginning to lose patience with you and your promises."

Monteith chuckled, his belly bouncing and jowls jiggling with his jubilance. "Aye. I told ye, Etherin'ton, I had done, but ye didna credit me."

"Where is it, then? I haven't all night." His eyebrows slashing low over his protuberant nose, the crow folded his arms. "As you know, my ship sails with the tide."

"I ken." Nodding, Monteith minced to the bookshelf to the right of the fireplace and removed four leather-bound burgundy volumes. "Ye'll be well-pleased," he boasted airily.

It baffled Bethea why a man his size opted to wear high heels and prance about on them. He looked utterly ridiculous.

He grunted a few times as he rummaged around in a hidden compartment behind the books before withdrawing a cylinder-shaped leather tube. A smug grin kicking his mouth up on one side, he pulled the cap off and extracted a rolled parchment. With a triumphant flourish, he waved the scroll in the air, a grin splitting the folds of his chuffy face.

A slow, utterly sinister smile pulled Etherington's mouth upward as he reached for the parchment. "It seems I underestimated you, Monteith."

The earl puffed his chest out, giving a superior nod. "It contains the signatures of every Scottish peer and laird vowin' their support in overthrowin' that German imposter sittin' upon the throne."

Once more, Bethea slapped a hand over her mouth to stifle her shocked gasp.

Traitors. They are both traitors.

She must inform Keane at once. He'd know what to do with the information.

Having lived in the Highlands and been sheltered by Keane, Bethea knew little of Scotland's politics. What she did know, however, was that plots such as this led to innocent people dying, clans dividing, and families splitting.

And much, *much* heartache and suffering.

"Well done. Well done, indeed." Scratching beneath his wig, Etherington gave a crackling, humorless chuckle. "I must be away, but I'll be in touch soon."

Monteith grunted, followed by a couple of *thunks*.

She presumed he replaced the books on the shelf.

"I need to return to my guests as well." He gave Etherington a sly glance. "I have my eye on a delectable lass I intend to make the next countess." He licked his fat lips and cupped his groin. "I've been hard as marble for a fortnight now, and the whores I've bedded havena relieved my lust. I canna wait to swive the girl. I'm positive she's a virgin, and ye ken I have a fondness for them."

Bile bubbled up Bethea's throat, and she swallowed reflexively against the sour burning.

"Mmm." Phillip Etherington made a noncommittal

sound as he tucked the folded parchment into an inner coat pocket. "Will she be your third or fourth countess?"

Third or fourth?

Bethea's stomach cramped, and bile throttled up her throat so swiftly that she thought she might be sick. Right there on the floor.

Monteith had been married that many times before?

And what, pray God, had happened to his other wives?

"The lass will be my fourth," Monteith said, not a hint of sorrow or remorse in his tone. "Two previous countesses died in childbirth and the last from a fever."

Well, that answered *that* question.

"I am desperate for an heir. Miss Bethea Glanville is young and healthy. Good, strong Highlander stock, rather than the insipid noble-borns with weak constitutions I've married before." Scratching his wide arse, Monteith pranced toward the door, passing wind as he went.

What a foul clod.

"You've asked for her hand, then?" Etherington picked a bit of lint from his sleeve, his demeanor revealing he didn't give a hog's fart about the subject. In truth, he seemed distracted. His mind elsewhere, that peculiar vacant gaze of his inching around the study.

Bethea changed her evaluation of him. He wasn't a crow at all, but rather a serpent.

"I mean to approach her guardian, and I'm confident he'll accept my suit." Monteith waited for Etherington to join him at the door. "If no', I havna a qualm about takin' her by force. Roxdale will come around then. If she's despoiled, he'll have nae choice."

Like hell, he willna.

A dozen agitated heartbeats later, the door snapped shut, and Bethea forced herself to slowly count to two hundred before she moved so much as a hair. Her mind whirled, and her heart beat frantically.

They needed to leave. Immediately. And then head straight back to the Highlands.

Determination in her step, she crossed the room and grasped the handle. But no sooner had she lowered the lever than Monteith and the snake violently shoved her back into the room.

Crying out in alarm and shock, Bethea stumbled backward several paces. Once she'd regained her balance, she drew herself up and met Monteith's leering gaze unflinchingly. Quite proud of her outward composure, she slid her focus to Etherington's stone-cold perusal.

Inwardly, she quaked like a newborn foal attempting to stand for the first time.

The earl advanced on her and seized her wrist in a cruel grip. "Och, I believe we may have found ourselves a spy, Etherin'ton."

"It certainly appears so," Etherington conceded in a disturbing monotone.

"Unhand me." Bethea jerked her arm free and cut the Englishman a swift glance. Her blood congealed at his lethal examination. She hadn't a doubt he'd see her dead if he supposed her an infiltrator.

Bethea shook her head.

"Ye're mistaken. I swear. My sister's in the retirin' room." She gestured vaguely toward the other door. "Her feet were injured dancin', and I was attemptin' to find a discreet way for her to leave without drawin' attention to her condition."

Upper lip curled, Etherington grunted his disbelief.

She forced a genial expression to her face and her tone of voice as she looked directly at Monteith. "Ye yerself saw us enter a few minutes ago, my lord."

Every word was true, which was a good thing, for Bethea was a poor liar.

Suspicion narrowing his eyes, Monteith rubbed his full jaw and nodded. "'Tis true."

A calculating expression crawled across Etherington's face. His frigid gunmetal eyes bored into her, demanding the truth, and it was all she could do not to avert her gaze. "But you listened to our conversation, didn't you?"

How could he know that?

She swallowed to wet her mouth, which had gone dry as ash. "I dinna ken what ye're talkin' about. I only just came through."

"*Tsk*, now you're lying, Miss Glanville." He examined a nail and scraped a bit of something from beneath it. Without raising his head, he directed his hooded gaze to her. "I heard your relieved sigh as we departed the chamber."

Had she sighed?

She didn't recall doing so.

He veered his attention to the door she'd hidden behind. "Had you been more careful, we never would've known."

Bethea cursed herself for a thousand kinds of careless fool. She should've headed straight back to the retiring room and sought Marjorie and Keane by way of that door.

Etherington flicked an icy, baleful glance over her. Head cocked, he touched a spindly finger to the deep cleft in his chin.

She had the absurd urge to laugh at the prominent dimple, which very much made his chin resemble a posterior. That feature seemed wholly incongruent with his sharply angled face.

"Now what to do with you?" he murmured, sending Monteith a questioning look.

"Ye are mistaken, sir." Bethea was so frightened she could

scarcely form the words. "As I said, I only now just came through here."

Monteith's pudgy features folded in contemplation as he leveled her a discerning look.

It was all Bethea could do not to retch. But she summoned her bravado and made to move past them. "If ye'll excuse me, gentlemen. My sister is waitin', and I promised my guardian I'd report on the condition of Branwen's feet. She's expectin' me."

What was another lie at this juncture?

In for a penny, in for a pound.

Marjorie had also said she'd check on her and Branwen.

How long ago was that?

Ten minutes? Fifteen?

Surely no more than twenty, which meant no one would come for them yet.

God help her.

"This works out quite well, actually, Etherin'ton." Monteith lumbered to the terrace doors and threw them open. "Take her with ye. It seems I shall have a new bride sooner than anticipated. And make sure nae one, and I mean *nae one*, touches her."

"You'll make it worth my while, of course," the Englishman murmured smoothly in that scraping voice that lifted Bethea's scalp hairs as he drifted nearer to her.

It wasn't a request.

"Of course," Monteith agreed heartily, scratching vigorously at his behind again.

Did he have fleas? Lice? *Something else?*

Bethea shuddered.

"I'm feelin' quite generous," the earl said, sliding his lewd gaze over Bethea.

"I can understand your fascination, Monteith. She truly is

a delectable little piece." Etherington's gaze dropped to her bosom, his mouth curving suggestively.

She shrank away, uncertain which man was more offensive.

"Dinna get any ideas," Monteith warned stonily, all pretense at civility gone. "She's mine."

Nae. This canna be happenin'.

"Nae—" Before Bethea finished her protest, Etherington struck her in the back of the head.

She felt herself falling, darkness closing in on her.

And then nothingness claimed her.

FIVE

Easter Road between Edinburgh and Leith
Just short of eleven o'clock
21 March 1721

His attention riveted on Easter Road, Camden hunched
further into his saddle. It was a bloody miserable night for
arresting traitors. Rivulets of rainwater dribbled from his nape
into his already sodden collar. But he'd experienced worse, and
the dampness proved a mere annoyance to a Highlander such
as himself.

He worked his astute gaze over his men strategically placed
along this section of the road. He knew from experience that
they were as keenly alert as him.

Unlike him, to a man, they thrived on the thrill—living on
the edge of danger. And also, unlike him and Bryston, not a
man amongst them could claim honor motivated his actions.
These dastards required a strong, uncompromising hand to
keep them in line.

If all went well, when this assignment culminated, the
mercenaries would receive the balance of their payment and

seek another employer with a heavy purse. Camden had put his foot down about working with such unpredictable and unsavory men in the future. Trained agents were one thing, but unreliable curs who'd as soon bite the hand that fed them as any other hand...

Nae, he was through with the lot, no matter what Sir Walter said.

In truth, as he'd never sought the dubious honor of spying on the King's behalf, he seriously considered another direction for his life as well.

Precisely what that looked like, he couldn't say.

He'd no desire to leave Scotland—permanently, at least. Oh, Graeme would claim to need Camden's help in overseeing his lairdship and their clan, but the truth was that his brother was more than capable of the task himself.

Younger sons often found themselves in predicaments like Camden's. He had no desire to enter the ministry or the military, nor did he particularly wish to travel the world for years. Nae, his heart was now and would always be in Scotland.

So, exactly, what the hell would he do with his time *if* he did resign?

And that brought him full circle to why he hadn't, as yet, done so.

Christ, his rambling musings scrambled *his* brain.

Swiping at a droplet trailing down his nose, he furrowed his brow, every sense tuned into the surroundings once more. In truth, he'd expected Etherington's coach by now. Another inspection of the track revealed only an empty black expanse unbroken by a single sliver of moonlight.

Perhaps Etherington had taken the Wester Road after all.

He mentally shrugged. It mattered not, as long as he was captured.

Bryston was just as capable as Camden of apprehending

the English conspirator and escorting him to the inn. As planned, they'd meet in the wee morning hours, and Etherington could explain himself to Sir Walter Makepeace.

After the revolt led by the Earl of Mar, Robert Walpole had personally selected Makepeace to head up the intelligence ring established for one purpose: to prevent any further uprisings in Scotland. And more importantly, to prevent further loss of life.

Lightly drumming his fingertips on his thigh, Camden hardened his jaw, his thoughts once more on Bethea.

He wouldn't wait to return to Trentwick Castle to speak with Keane about Monteith's interest in her. In fact, it might be worthwhile to also have that devil's spawn investigated.

After all, why, precisely, was Etherington even invited to his ball?

Had he been invited?

Perhaps not, which begged the question, why would Etherington overstep propriety and impose himself? It wasn't as if he held a lofty title, and none would dare object to his presence.

Except, to Camden's knowledge, Monteith hadn't raised a fuss, and he knew the answer to why Etherington was present. To obtain a very valuable list. A list incriminating every Scottish conspirator, signed in their own hands.

Idiots all.

Last month, Bryston had proposed Monteith as a possible collaborator. Sir Walter, however, had immediately dismissed the notion. He'd emphatically claimed the earl all but kissed King George's arse each time he saw him. Monteith had never openly associated with anyone suspected of disloyalty to the Crown either.

Until now.

Still, the stark apprehension and fear Camden witnessed

ravaging Bethea's face earlier this evening made him determined to remove her from Monteith's reach, no matter what it took.

Keane should never have brought the Glanville sisters to Edinburgh. They should've remained safe in the Highlands, where whoremongers like the Earl of Monteith couldn't prey upon them.

In the distance, the distinct rumble and creak of coach wheels and the unmistakable rhythmic clopping of hoofbeats filtered through the damp night air. *At last.* Camden straightened and gave a low bird whistle, signaling his men to be at the ready.

In addition to a dirk and sword, each man also carried at least one loaded blunderbuss. They'd avoided bloodshed waylaying the previous coaches in search of incriminating evidence, but that didn't mean there wouldn't be a first time.

Nevertheless, Etherington must be taken alive.

Camden didn't fool himself into believing Sir Walter or another of the king's lackeys, delegators, or advisors wouldn't torture the traitor to get the information they wanted.

Etherington wasn't acting alone, of that Camden had no doubt. Unquestionably, more Englishmen were involved as well. It was no secret George I wasn't liked by the English any more than he was by the Scots. Most considered him an imposter who could scarcely speak English and preferred to spend his time in Hanover.

According to a double agent, someone had acquired the signatures of Scots willing to overthrow George I. Just who that someone was, only Etherington's accomplice knew for certain.

The collaborator was cunning. He never met directly with anyone and always passed his messages through a string of contacts. And he never used the same messengers twice.

Yet, the conspirator had grown sloppy in the last two weeks. Word had leaked that tonight Etherington would acquire the very damning list.

God help any Scot who'd put their signature to it.

It was as good as a confession.

At best, they faced imprisonment. At worst, the rebels would lose their heads. The Crown would confiscate everything they owned, and quite likely imprison or put to death anyone associated with the traitors, whether they were guilty or not.

A frog croaked and then another and then another. In short order, hundreds of frogs' mating calls filled the night. The sound was slightly haunting and captivating.

The outline of a vehicle lumbering down Easter Road came into view. Its two exterior lamps sent peculiar shadows cavorting with each bump and rattle of the coach.

Camden kicked Prometheus's sides and guided the huge horse to the center of the lane. He removed his blunderbuss from his waistband and rested it casually across the top of his thighs. From the corner of his eyes, he watched in satisfaction as his men stealthily moved into place.

As they had the previous times, they'd surround the coach, making escape impossible.

No moon lit the sky, but the layer of clouds had parted here and there, allowing a glimpse of a few twinkling stars.

When the coach was within a few feet of him, Camden stood in his saddle, raised his pistol, and pointed it directly at the coachmen.

The coach lamps swayed violently as the conveyance jerked to an abrupt halt. Even in the dim light, Camden couldn't miss the pallor of the frightened drivers' faces.

The men offered no resistance whatsoever. After

exchanging alarmed glances, they raised their hands overhead, fear etching deep grooves into their faces.

That said much about the man riding in comfort inside the conveyance. A well-treated employee was a loyal employee and protected his employer. This pair hadn't hesitated to surrender.

"Why have we stopped?" An arrogant, grating English voice cut through the night. A moment later, three firm raps echoed on the coach roof. "I asked why we have stopped? I have a ship to catch before the tide turns."

Etherington was such an arrogant ass.

He hadn't even bothered with outriders, convinced that no one suspected him of his treasonous activities.

His men had guided their mounts into position. A horseman flanked either side of the vehicle, and a rider guarded the rear of the vehicle as well.

Wordlessly, Camden motion for the drivers to descend. The coach bounced and groaned as they climbed down without hesitation. Once on the ground, the coachmen tore off on foot, never once glancing back.

Indeed, Etherington must be a royal prig for his men to abandon him so readily.

A string of vile curses echoed from within the conveyance. Etherington was no lackwit and must've deduced what was happening. "Damned riff-raff. I'll see every one of you bastards hanged. Drawn and quartered. Bloody highwaymen."

Camden grinned, despite the seriousness of the situation.

If Etherington was such a brave fellow, why was he still sequestered inside the coach?

After throwing one leg over Prometheus's side, Camden slid to the ground.

His men followed suit, except for the rider at the rear. He'd give chase if required.

Blunderbuss at the ready, Camden edged closer. Only a fool rushed ahead without knowing exactly what he faced.

Sir Phillip Etherington mightn't be alone, or he might be armed.

Before Camden could open the door himself, the panel swung outward, and the crow-like man pushed his narrow shoulders into the opening. "What is the meaning of this?" he demanded, all pompous outrage.

At Camden's signal, his men also aimed their pistols directly at Etherington. With mufflers wrapped around their faces and only their eyes visible, Camden didn't fear recognition. Though, in truth, he doubted the mercenaries cared about concealing their identities. Just as long as they received the rest of their coin when this was over, they'd be satisfied.

As satisfied as anyone with no conscience or moral code could be.

Craning his neck, Etherington scowled ferociously at the empty drivers' seat, then brought his infuriated gaze back to Camden and sneered. "Bloody cowards. They didn't even put up a fight."

"I do have to wonder why," Camden drolly observed, earning him a loathing-filled glare. "Show yer hands," he ordered.

Etherington didn't immediately comply.

"Ye should ken, three weapons are trained on ye. One false move, and it will be yer last." Camden wasn't foolish enough to underestimate the man.

Etherington's expression grew more disdainful as he pursed his mouth and glowered at each gunman in turn. "You realize, of course, I wouldn't be foolish enough to carry a large purse with me."

Camden remained silent and cocked a brow mockingly, having learned long ago that nervous people often prattled.

And for all of Phillip Etherington's bravado, he was as nervous as a new whore.

Etherington swore beneath his breath as he began fiddling inside his coat pocket.

"I said, show yer hands. Now." Camden bit out the last, leveling the barrel of his pistol directly at Etherington's chest.

Eyes narrowed, his sunken features taut, Etherington slowly withdrew his hand from his coat. He clutched a small leather purse in his fist but obediently extended his hands. "I'm not armed. I was but retrieving my purse."

"We're no' interested in yer money," Camden said, convinced more than ever that the damning documents were concealed within the coach.

Else why would Etherington voluntarily come out and offer his purse?

He'd also wager Prometheus that a weapon or two lay within the vehicle. Camden jerked his pistol in a manner indicating Etherington should descend from the conveyance. "Get out."

Etherington scowled sinisterly, his gaze shifting from gun to gun.

"There's no need for me to descend." He threw his coin purse onto the ground near Camden's feet. "I haven't any other valuables on me," he declared. "Take it and be gone with you, bastards."

Then he proceeded to spit, indicating his contempt.

"Does the sot truly think we'd believe him?" One of the men chuckled.

They were only too eager for a bit of sport. Etherington had better comply or he'd be the worse for it.

They knew nothing of the document or Camden's real reason for robbing Etherington. Greedy lot that they were, they assumed the real valuables lay within the coach.

"I said, out." Camden stepped forward. "Ye can do so of yer own accord, or I'll have my men drag ye. Yer choice."

"I'm just returning from a business meeting. As you can well see, I don't even have luggage with me," Etherington grumbled as he stepped from the conveyance. He made a point of closing the door behind him. "I don't have any more coin on me either."

As if that would keep Camden from searching the vehicle from top to bottom. He would dismantle the damn thing, if necessary. He was convinced the documentation that would prove Etherington's guilt, as well as those conspiring against the Crown, lay within the vehicle somewhere.

At once, his men stepped forward and constrained Etherington by either arm.

He struggled, swearing and shouting dire threats the entire time. "I'm a citizen of England and an advisor to the king himself. He won't take kindly to you maltreating me."

Tucking his blunderbuss into his waistband, Camden nodded toward Etherington. "Tie and gag him."

"I've told you I haven't any other valuables with me." He strained against the men holding him. "Except... I do have a gold watch. You can have that too."

"Nae, thanks," Camden said, sauntering forward. "I have my own."

Etherington's rather creative curses filled the night air and then abruptly ceased. Angry, muffled noises followed.

As his men went about their tasks of restraining the traitor, Camden jerked the coach door open.

Holy hell.

His heart ceased beating as his mind tried to comprehend and accept what his eyes clearly saw.

Shite. Shite. Shite.

Slumped in the corner, bound and gagged, and wearing

only her ballgown and no cloak, Bethea Glanville lay unconscious.

He whirled around, a feral snarl pulling his lips back from his teeth.

His fingers twitched with the urge to wrap around the bugger's skinny throat.

"What the hell is *she* doin' here?" he demanded, stabbing a finger toward the coach. He marched over to Etherington, sitting on the ground, and jerked the gag down. "I'll give ye one chance to answer me. And one chance only. Why is Bethea Glanville in yer coach?"

As one, his men's attention veered to the open door, and Anderson meandered a few feet closer to get a better look. The worst whoremonger of the bunch. The man had a constant itch between his legs that no amount of swiving satisfied.

Damnation.

A much fouler expletive knocked at the back of his teeth.

His men hankering after Bethea Glanville was the last thing Camden needed. He'd dismiss Anderson this very moment and send him on his way, but he didn't trust the churl not to retaliate to save face. Of all the mercenaries, Anderson possessed the most pride and arrogance.

Etherington's perceptive gaze narrowed as his regard shifted between Camden and the open carriage door. "Ah, you know the girl?"

Camden felt every man's eyes swing to him.

"Now, that *is* fascinating." A sly smile tipped his almost non-existent lips upward at the corners. "Monteith means to make her his bride, you know," he remarked, almost conversationally.

Over my dead body.

"I'm to meet him in Northumberland in six days." He lifted a brow. "But...perhaps, *we* can come to an agreement?"

Camden would kill Monteith if Keane didn't get to him first.

"She's a lovely bit of fluff," Anderson observed with a lusty grin. "This job just became considerably more interestin'."

Exchanging a knowing look with his compatriots, he winked as his lewd grin widened.

Hands on his hips, Camden rotated to face his men straight on, his mind racing. They'd not hesitate to ravish Bethea unless they feared severe repercussions. She was an unexpected benefit, and they'd not take kindly to having their lust denied.

"Watch yer mouth, Anderson. She's nae *bit of fluff*. She's my cousin, the Duke of Roxdale's ward." He cursed inwardly. That would mean nothing to them except perhaps an opportunity to demand a ransom for her.

Anderson lifted a shoulder dismissively. "That disna mean we canna have a bit of fun. Right lads?"

Lecherous leers kicked the other mercenaries' mouths upward. "Never had me a lady before," one murmured, ogling Bethea. He licked his lips and adjusted his cock.

Sweet Jesus on Sunday.

"I'd say you have an unanticipated problem." Etherington chuckled evilly, and Camden balled his fists to keep from slugging him. A punch to his nose could only improve the appendage.

These men were laws unto themselves, and the only way he could protect Bethea was claiming her as his own.

Hell and damnation.

"She's also *my* betrothed." He splayed his legs and looked at each man in turn. "I'll no' hesitate to kill any man who looks at her with anythin' but respect, never mind one stupid enough to touch her."

Mutinous grumbles followed his declaration.

"Do ye understand?" Heart thundering, he met each disgruntled man's gaze in turn. "She is *mine*. If any of ye object to waitin' to relieve yerself with a whore, then ye can take yer leave. However, I do understand yer disappointment, and there are an extra ten pounds apiece to any man who stays."

Sir Walter had forced these sods upon him, and he could pay the extra fee.

A round of cheers went up. These rotters loved nothing— *nothing*—more than coin.

"But she's such a prime little mort." Etherington cackled again, and this time Camden did punch him. He flew backward, legs and arms splayed, reinforcing his crow-like appearance. "Count yerself fortunate that I didna slay ye myself."

Holding a hand to his spurting nose, Etherington glared at Camden. "Your superior will hear about this."

God's ballocks! And still, he blathers.

A cold smile curved Camden's mouth as he bent over the cowering Englishman. "I only have to deliver ye alive. What condition ye are in is up to me. My inclination, at present, is to beat ye into a bloody pulp." With that, he straightened and, with deliberate nonchalance, sauntered toward the coach.

His men chuckled. They also enjoyed violence.

Puzzling his forehead, he tried for the umpteenth time to comprehend why Sir Walter insisted on using such degenerates rather than soldiers or agents.

SIX

Road to Dalkeith
Early morning
22 March 1721

Bethea groaned and cautiously moved her throbbing head.

What had happened?

She tried to recall, even as she realized from the rumbling wheels and rhythmic swaying that she was in a vehicle.

Take her with ye. She's mine.

Monteith!

Recollection flooded her. Terror curdling her blood, she bolted upright, crying out as pain lanced the back of her head.

Sweet Jesus, Mary, and Joseph.

She stifled a moan but only just.

"Shh, lass, yer safe now." A large hand briefly rested on her shoulder, warm and reassuring.

Not the Etherington's bony appendage, nor his British accent, which sounded like he'd gargled glass shards.

Through the fog of confusion and fear, recognition took root.

Bethea knew that rich, comforting burr.

Camden Kennedy?

But how? Why?

Her stomach roiled violently, and she allowed her eyelids to drift closed for a blink.

Och, God above, she might be sick.

Swallowing nausea climbing her throat, she touched her fingertips to the aching throb at the base of her skull. A combination of the vehicle's movements and the blow to her head made vomiting a very real possibility.

Confused, refusing to believe her eyes, she cowered in the corner shaking. But not from the cold. Someone had put an oversized, slightly damp coat on her.

His coat.

It smelled slightly of wet wool and a lighter, musky scent. A manly aroma hinting of the outdoors, pine trees, and mayhap—she gave a light sniff—mayhap *cloves*?

Camden had retreated a few inches, concern lining his face and crinkling the corner of his indigo eyes. "Did he harm ye?"

What...? What was *he* doing here?

"Camden?"

She blinked several times, trying to clear the cobwebs from her fuzzy brain—attempting to remember precisely what had happened.

Squinting, she envisioned the Earl of Monteith's ballroom.

Branwen had injured her feet while dancing. Well, that clodpole Lord Hurstwood had tromped upon her toes, bruising them quite grievously.

Yes, and then Bethea was supposed to have found Marjorie and Keane and another, less visible, way to leave the ball.

Brow puckered, she brushed her fingertips back and forth over the soft wool of his coat.

The memories came swifter now.

She'd been in Monteith's study.

Fear speared her.

He'd ordered that foul Englishman to take her with him.

Her throat tightened in renewed horror. Her breathing irregular, she clutched her neck.

Oh, God.

Monteith meant to force her into a marriage.

He'd said he'd violate her.

Another wave of sickness assailed her at the thought.

Then pain had exploded at the back of her head. Etherington must've struck her, the fiend.

She had no idea how she'd come to be in this coach with Camden. Suspicion she didn't want to acknowledge, let alone entertain, lanced her, and she retreated deeper into the corner.

What if, God forbid, *he* was working with Etherington and Monteith?

Ludicrous.

But—was it?

Camden wasn't supposed to be at the ball, and yet he had been. And he hadn't told anyone he'd be there. He'd also seen her helping Branwen into the retiring room.

Why, exactly, had he been standing behind Monteith?

Waiting for an opportunity to speak with him, mayhap? To conspire against the Crown? But wouldn't he then have also joined Monteith and Etherington in the study?

"Bethea?" Concern deepened Camden's rich brogue and drew his midnight eyebrows into a severe vee. He reached out to touch her, but when she flinched away, he allowed his hand to fall into his lap.

"Lass?" he asked tentatively and soothingly, as one would an injured, frightened animal. "Are ye all right? Did...?" He cleared his throat, his expression becoming quite fierce. "Did Etherin'ton hurt ye?"

Hurt me?

Och, he means—

Her cheeks burned at his implication.

"He hit me in the back of the head, but that's all."

At least she thought it was. How, however, could she be certain?

Closing her eyes, Bethea inhaled even breaths and took a mental inventory. She didn't hurt anywhere but her head—no sore muscles or bruises or aches in unmentionable places.

Monteith had been most avid that she was to remain untouched.

Nae, she was positive, Etherington hadn't imposed himself upon her.

Nonetheless, she knitted her forehead in befuddlement as she opened her eyes and scrutinized Camden.

Why was he here?

Call her foolish, but she was still unwilling to accept that the laughing, considerate man who'd attended Keane's Hogmanay celebration had anything to do with her abduction. Or the plot against the Crown.

"He struck ye?" Camden swore beneath his breath, striking a fist to his knee. A feral scowl contorted his handsome features for a heartbeat before he arranged them into a less intimidating mien. "He'll pay for that, by God. Pay dearly for layin' a hand on ye, lass. I'll make sure of it."

So would Keane.

There'd not be much left of Etherington or Monteith by the time those two finished with them. She couldn't summon an iota of pity.

Bethea surreptitiously examined Camden. He'd changed his clothes since the ball and now wore all jet black, except for his shirt. A simple knitted black cap covered his sable hair as well. He looked like a humble laborer or a farmhand.

How had he come to be in this coach with her, and where were Sir Phillip Etherington and Monteith?

There was only one way to find out.

Yes, she might not know where she was, or how she would escape, but she wasn't so hen-hearted she'd not ask. This was her life, after all.

She'd craved excitement and adventure, but this assuredly wasn't what she'd had in mind.

"Why?" The word came out a raspy croak. "Why are ye here?" Bethea swallowed again, her waffy stomach less overwhelming but present nonetheless. "Where's that despicable Englishman and the Earl of Monteith?"

Bethea darted an uneasy glance toward a window.

Out there?

Nae, Camden *wasn't* working with them.

He couldn't be.

He wouldn't hurt her. She instinctively knew it.

Knew that he was good at his core, as much as Monteith was evil to the depths of his black soul. *God rot him.*

In fact, at Trentwick, she'd suspected Camden might, in fact, esteem her. In the way a man admires a woman who's captured his serious masculine interest.

Bethea had been flattered, quite naturally.

How could she not be?

Camden was dashing, possessed a physique a Roman god might envy, and was handsome in the rugged way many Highlanders were. He was also a tease and a flirt, and seldom took anything seriously.

He'd not said a word, of course, and she couldn't very well ask what his reputation was with the ladies. Instinct told her he had no detriments on that front, and if she began poking around making inquiries about a handsome Kennedy, Keane wouldn't take it well.

A thread of tension yet remained between the Kennedys and Buchannans, and he knew full well how blasted protective Keane was of her and Branwen.

Her dreams of partaking in Edinburgh's high social season had remained firmly affixed in her mind. She'd not settle on the first Highlander that paid her any attention when she might very well meet a gentleman who'd steal her heart and sweep her off her feet in Edinburgh.

What did she truly know of Camden Kennedy?

Certainly not that he appeared at balls unannounced, dressed for stealthy activities, or mysteriously wound up in coaches in the middle of the night.

An almost wry smile quirked his mouth, and the rakish glint she knew so well twinkled in his eyes.

Surprisingly—or perhaps foolishly—his rapscallion charm relaxed her.

Kicking his legs out before him and crossing his booted ankles, he reclined against the seat. Arms folded, the ridiculously muscled cords straining against the lucky fabric of his roughly woven shirt, he jutted his strong chin toward the back of the coach. A chin, she couldn't help but notice, shadowed by dark stubble.

"Etherin'ton, the bastard, is gagged and tied to a horse. The horse, in turn, is secured to the back of this coach." He gave a decidedly wicked chuckle, and a little thrill jolted through her.

He truly did have the most delicious voice. The kind that made a woman want to lay her head against the broad expanse of his chest and listen to the vibrations when he spoke.

Good God. Where had that twaddle originated?

Perchance, Etherington had struck her harder than she'd realized and addled her.

"As 'tis rainin' steadily, he wasna overly pleased on bein'

denied the comfort of the coach. Monteith, I presume, is still in Edinburgh, although he's supposed to collect ye from Etherin'ton in a few days."

They must've plotted that while she was unconscious.

Camden cut a glance at the black night sky. "I dinna ken what their specific arrangements were, and Etherin'ton isna exactly being forthcomin' on the matter after I broke his nose."

He'd broken Etherington's nose? Good for him.

What time was it, anyway?

Branwen, Marjorie, and Keane would be frantic by now.

Tears burned behind her eyelids.

Branwen would blame herself.

Resolutely, Bethea blinked the moisture away. Naught could be done now. She'd fret about that later, and perhaps how to contrive a means of getting a message to them as well. Right now, she must focus on these dire circumstances.

She slid Camden a furtive glance beneath her lashes.

"Camden, I'm verra confused." She gathered his coat tighter around her. "How did ye come to be here?"

She tried to keep her voice steady, but an inflection of suspicion and misgivings colored her question.

He heard the nuance, and disbelief illuminated his gaze before his blue eyes became shuttered. He ripped the cap from his head and tossed it on the seat, the line of his mouth grim. "I canna tell ye everythin', lass. But I can vow ye'll be safe with me."

"Are ye a smuggler?" She'd heard whispers that he was but had dismissed them as rubbish. *Now, however...*

One raven eyebrow arched, and then he astonished her by chuckling. "Aye, I used to be. Also a marauder, but only when directed by His Majesty." He gave her a devilish wink.

Good God, was he a *spy?*

Was he trying to shock her?

She'd had quite enough shock for one day, thank you very much.

"Camden, be serious. Right now, it verra much appears that ye are part of the conspiracy to see me ravished by Monteith." She sucked in a calming breath. "I am havin' a difficult time believin' that about ye—"

"Och, thank ye for that." He cut her a curt glance and appeared genuinely offended.

"What else am I supposed to think?" She threw a hand up and immediately regretted the sudden motion when her aching skull soundly objected. "The last thing I remember was Monteith tellin' Etherin'ton to take me with him, and he'd make it worth his while."

"Nae, I'm nae conspirator. Set yer mind at ease about that." Camden scraped a big hand through his hair. "Sir Phillip Etherin'ton *is* a traitor, however, and I'm turnin' him over to an English agent awaitin' us. That's all I can tell ye. I'm sorry."

Her lower lip caught between her teeth, she probed his gaze. Either he was a fantastical liar, or he spoke the truth.

She'd bet her life on the latter, and her instinct had never steered her wrong before. But then again, she'd never been abducted and awoken to a spy reassuring her.

The list!

Bethea had almost forgotten.

She leaned forward and earnestly clasped his hand resting atop his marbled thigh. "Etherin'ton has a list. The names of peers and...and others who have vowed to depose the king."

Camden looked at her incredulously. "How do ye ken that?"

"I saw Monteith give it to him. He took it from a secret

compartment hidden behind books in his study." She quickly relayed what had happened.

"Och, now that is verra interestin' indeed." An approving smile tilted his mouth. "Well done. Ye've uncovered the contact we've been seekin' for the better part of a year, Bethea."

"I have?" A surge of pride engulfed her.

"Indeed. Ye've helped save many lives." He gathered her much smaller hand in his.

She wasn't altogether certain that excitement that she'd helped catch a spy was causing the heat infusing her or the quivering in her belly.

"But I need ye to swear no' to tell anyone else of this until I tell ye 'tis safe to do so."

Unease reared its head. "Why?"

He angled his dark head toward the outdoors again. His hair hung to his shoulders and swung slightly with the motion. "I have three hired men with me. Untrustworthy, unsavory curs who'd sell that information, no' carin' the lives it would cost or the havoc it would wreak on Scotland."

She gulped and slid an apprehensive glance in the direction he'd looked. "Why are they with ye if they are so disloyal and reprehensible?"

He turned her hand over, examining her palm.

Where were her gloves?

Oh, that's right, she'd removed them when caring for Branwen.

"They are the best at what they do," he replied, matter of factly. "That's all ye need to ken."

She studied his face for a long moment.

Nae, I didna ken Camden Kennedy at all.

Camden's jaw flexed, and he gently squeezed her fingers. "How is yer head?"

"Sore, and there's a mighty lump." Bethea gingerly probed her scalp. It wasn't bleeding, so she supposed she ought to be grateful for that small blessing.

He made a harsh sound in his throat. "Do ye feel waffy or dizzy?"

"Only sick at my stomach, but that might be from the coach. I get sick on long journeys. 'Tis the rockin' motion. 'Tis the same on boats too." She gave him a rueful smile. "I fear I'm no' exactly heroine material."

"Och, that depends on who the hero is, disna it?" His voice held a tone she couldn't quite identify but which sent a delicious thrill through her.

And, at present, she wasn't in any mind to examine it further. "What time is it? My family will be beside themselves, and that fat pissant is to blame."

"It's nearly half-past two." He gave her hand a slight squeeze. Odd, she had no desire to remove it from his warm clasp. "We'll send word to Keane as soon as possible. I promise ye."

"I wonder how that asslin' Monteith explained my disappearance?"

Camden didn't look shocked at her use of profanity. "I'd guess he vowed ignorance and put on a show of concern worthy of a Shakespearian actor."

Sighing, she rested against the surprisingly comfortable squabs. "I'm beginnin' to wish I'd never left the Highlands."

He seemed distracted and only tipped his mouth on one side at her declaration.

"Bethea?"

She turned her head, exhaustion weighing her eyelids. "Aye?"

"We'll arrive at our destination soon." Something shadowed the contours of Camden's face, but she couldn't identify what it was. If she had to put a word to it, the expression had been something between regret and resignation.

"Bethea?" he said her name again.

She went still, searching his face. "There's somethin' else, isna there?"

Almost bashfully, he scratched his eyebrow and gave a slow nod. "I had to claim that ye... To keep the men from..." Jaw flexing, he released a gust of breath. "That is, to assure yer safety and that nae one dare impose their—ah—attentions on ye, I had to claim ye were my betrothed."

Bethea, again, glanced out the window, unable to see the riders accompanying them. Camden wouldn't have made such an assertion if it hadn't been necessary.

"I suppose it could've been worse," she bantered. "Ye could've said I was yer wife, and in Scotland, that might be enough to be considered an irregular marriage."

SEVEN

The Boar and Brew Inn and Tavern
Dalkeith, Scotland
22 March 1721

Bloody damned hell.

Camden gritted his teeth to tame more curses as he handed Bethea down from the coach onto the sodden ground. To a man, his men stared at her like she was a sweetmeat or a dainty they wanted to gobble up. For her part, she kept her gaze averted and stayed close to his side.

She might not admit it, but her trembling revealed her unease.

The rain had ceased, but the air remained damp and heavy with the promise of more showers.

Though Sir Walter awaited his arrival, he'd see Bethea settled in a chamber first. A locked chamber. He'd appoint a guard as well, but he didn't trust anyone besides himself and Bryston.

As if conjured by his thoughts, Bryston McPherson appeared in the inn's doorway. His eyes went wide upon

73

spying Bethea, but after Camden's infinitesimal shake of his head, Bryston gravitated his attention to Etherington.

"Take him inside. I'll be there momentarily."

With a curt nod, Bryston clasped a soggy, sweaty, white-faced Etherington. His swollen nose had begun to bruise already. They disappeared inside the inn, and several men turned curious glances on Bethea, bold male interest and appreciation in their eyes.

With her sable hair, bowed mouth—red from nervously chewing her lower lip—gently sloping cheeks, and dove-gray, almond-shaped eyes beneath winged eyebrows set in an oval face, she was unquestionably lovely.

His coat hid most of her womanly assets, but he knew her to have a narrow waist, nipped in by stays, and a full, creamy bosom. He also knew she smelled of lilacs and lilies.

When he'd put his coat on her, her perfume had teased him unmercifully.

Camden had best get her inside and out of their view. No sense tempting the men with what they couldn't have.

"Anderson and Headden, take care of the horses and then have yerselves somethin' to eat." The hostler had been paid in advance to have food, drink, and their rooms prepared for their arrival.

Pray to God, a chamber was available for Bethea that bolted from inside.

At least a dozen uniformed soldiers lounged about the common room as Camden steered Bethea inside by her elbow.

Tension radiated off her in undulating waves.

"Easy, sweet," he whispered in her ear. "Nae harm will come to ye."

Glancing upward, she summoned a wan smile.

"I'll see ye settled in a chamber before I meet with my contact," he murmured.

The slim column of her throat worked, but she managed a stiff nod.

Once inside the inn, and after speaking with Shamus Dowdery, the innkeeper, Camden swore a vile oath.

Bloody hell.

No additional rooms were available.

There was no help for it. Bethea would have to use his. There was no way she could stay in the common area with this many men about, and she couldn't be present for his confidential meeting with Sir Walter Makepeace.

"I'll need a dinner tray and hot water sent up at once," he told Shamus, a cheerful chap, despite the ungodly hour and the two score unruly men crowding his establishment.

"Aye. My missus will see to it." He motioned a beefy arm toward the thrumming common room. "The barmaids are a bit overwhelmed at present."

Even at this hour, the place buzzed with conversation and laughter.

Camden escorted her to the chamber assigned to him. Leaving the door ajar, he swiftly lit a lamp and nodded his approval. Small and humble, but clean. A bed took up most of the room, an extra quilt folded across the foot. On one side of the bed stood a washstand, and on the other, a chair. A single window, the shutters closed and barred from within, was centered in the wall across from the bed.

As this was the third story, no one would be entering that way. He closed the door, and after inspecting the sturdy bar that acted as a detriment to unwanted visitors, he cupped her shoulders.

Her eyes huge in her pale face, she gazed at him with such trust that it humbled him.

"I have to leave ye, Bethea."

A sharp rap portended the mistress of the establishment's

entrance. "My, but 'tis a busy one," she said, blustering into the already cramped chamber. She set the tray upon the chair and motioned for a teenage lad to pour steaming water into the basin from the pail he held.

"Thank you," Bethea said with a generous smile for both of them. "The food smells delicious."

She'd always done that—had a ready smile for everyone and made everyone feel special. Mayhap she'd been too polite to Monteith, and he'd mistaken her kindness for something more.

Mrs. Dowerdy beamed. "There's soap and linen on the washstand." She wiped her hands on her apron before pushing several strands of wispy dark blonde hair under her cap. "If ye havna need of anythin' else, I'll go below. Those soldiers seem to think my girls are available for purchase." She sniffed disapprovingly. "I'm a God-fearin' woman, and I run a respectable establishment."

She cast Camden a gimlet eye before her less than subtle gaze slid to Bethea. He'd told her husband Bethea was his betrothed, but her lack of a chaperone or maid certainly made that assertion suspicious. Not to mention, she still wore his coat.

Bethea gave him a helpless little glance.

"Thank ye." Camden produced a coin, and that seemed to mollify the woman.

She took herself off, giving the weary lad orders as they departed.

"Bar the door and dinna open it for anyone but me," Camden said. "If I can manage it, I'll send Bryston up to guard the door."

Bethea nodded as she sank onto the bed and put a hand to her injured head. "How long will ye be?"

He shook his head. "I have nae idea. Try to eat somethin' and then rest."

"I shan't be able to sleep a wink, but I am hungry." She lifted the cloth covering the tray and smiled. "Scotch pies." She held two out to him. "Here, ye must be starvin' too."

He gratefully accepted them with one hand and drew her close with the other. He dropped a kiss onto her forehead in what he hoped was a brotherly fashion. What she stirred in him was most certainly not fraternal, but there was no time to explore that now.

Sir Walter awaited him, and the king's advisor was not a patient man.

Camden stepped from the chamber and drew the door partially shut. "Secure it after me."

Taking a bite of the savory pie, he waited until he heard the bar slam home before heading below, gulping down the remaining pie as he went. He needed a pint of ale now.

Hell, a bottle of whisky wouldn't go amiss.

He might've saved Bethea from Etherington and Monteith's despicable plans for her, but how in Odin's teeth could he salvage her reputation?

He couldn't.

Ruined.

That was what she was.

Utterly and irrevocably.

Even before he brought her to the inn, she'd been beyond redemption. Merely being alone with Etherington was enough to cause a scandal, and then she'd been alone with Camden. And now two score men, as well as Dowerdy and his wife, had seen her.

An astute lass, surely Bethea understood how perilous her situation was.

Camden didn't want to contemplate Keane's reaction.

Keane was the product of rape and a forced marriage. He'd come unhinged if he thought Bethea had come to harm, or if a hint of scandal or impropriety was associated with her name.

Even Camden wasn't entirely certain he'd be safe from Keane's vengeance, though he'd rescued Bethea from the devious plans Monteith had for her.

As he made his way to the parlor reserved for the appointment with Sir Walter Makepeace, he turned his thoughts to the list tucked inside his boot. He'd found it after a thorough search of Etherington's person.

The idiot hadn't even bothered to try to hide it in the coach.

His arrogance had been his downfall in more ways than one.

Two weary red-clad soldiers stood guard outside the private parlor. They gave him curious glances but remained silent as he knocked briskly.

Knock. Knock. Knock.

After receiving a curt request to enter, he strode into the room.

Bryston was already there, resting a shoulder against the wall. He dipped his chin in a wordless greeting.

Standing before the fireplace, Sir Walter Makepeace examined a document. Barely six inches over five feet and so slight he looked as if a strong wind might blow him over, many were the fools who'd underestimated the advisor. A brilliant strategist possessing a keen intelligence, he had the king's ear for a reason. As was his habit, he wore a gray jacket and breeches. Only his waistcoat ever changed color. Today, it was a dark green and ebony striped affair.

He acknowledged Camden's entrance with a penetrating glance and a sharp nod before his attention veered to Etherington.

Three bored, heavy-lidded soldiers stood guard near the traitorous Englishman.

As if an honored guest, Phillip Etherington sat picking at a plate of food, a serviette tucked into his collar, his nose a swollen beacon in his face. The simple fare might well be his last meal.

Camden would've let the cur starve, and he couldn't help but wonder at the traitor's preferential treatment. Did Makepeace think treating Etherington civilly would loosen his tongue?

The smile Etherington slid Camden raised the hairs on his scalp.

Leaning back, Etherington nonchalantly took a sip of wine. "I was explaining to Sir Walter how your *betrothed* happened to be in my company."

His tone indicated he clearly didn't believe Bethea and Camden were trothed.

Bryston went perfectly still, but like any agent worth his salt, his expression didn't reveal his astonishment. He, of course, knew damn well Camden was no more affianced to Bethea Glanville than he was able to sprout wings and fly back to the Highlands.

Arms folded, Camden regarded the Englishmen with the same favor he would a corpse fished from the North Sea after a month. "Did ye also tell him why ye agreed to abduct her so that Monteith could violate her, and thereby force her to wed him?"

Slowly straightening to his impressive six feet four inches, Bryston wrapped his hand around the handle of the dirk at his waist. The look he exchanged with Camden spoke volumes.

He also well knew Keane's fury, and if Sir Walter didn't dispose of Etherington and Monteith, Keane would. Bryston tipped his hawkish gaze toward the ceiling in silent communication, and Camden answered with a barely discernable movement of his eyes.

Without a word, Bryston slipped from the room.

Bethea would be safe until Camden returned.

Sir Walter, a devotedly religious man—fanatical some would say—looked appropriately appalled. "Contemptible behavior." He turned his sad, hound dog brown-eyed gaze upon Camden. "How fares your affianced? Is she overwrought? Is there anything I can do to ease her distress?"

"She's restin' in my room." The less Sir Walter knew about Bethea, the better. He wasn't above exploiting the situation if he thought it in any way might be used to bring him favor with His Majesty.

In truth, he'd pondered several times why Robert Walpole had chosen Sir Walter to head the uprising suppressions. Makepeace's political experience leaned toward commerce and foreign affairs, rather than civil rebellion.

"Good. Good." With a slant of his head and an extended arm, he indicated Camden should precede him into an adjoining room. Once out of Etherington's earshot, Sir Walter asked, "Have you the documentation?"

Camden bent and pulled the paper from his boot. Wordlessly, he passed it to the advisor.

"Have you read it?"

Camden shook his head. "Nae. Ye said 'twas classified."

With an affirmative grunt, Makepeace unfurled the parchment, his white, wiry eyebrows contorting as he read the list of names. Rather than gloating or celebratory, he raised those soulful eyes to Camden's. "A bloody shame." He tapped the paper. "Good men here. Good men caught up in misplaced loyalty."

"Aye." Sighing, Camden cupped his nape. It brought him no joy or sense of satisfaction to have succeeded at his assignment. Fellow Scots would lose their lives, and that was never a cause for rejoicing. "And as ye may have deduced already, Monteith is the other rat we've been after."

Sir Walter crinkled his broad brow and set his full mouth into a stern line. "I confess, I still find that galling to accept." He tapped the paper with a forefinger again. "In all these years I've been at this business, it still grieves me to learn of the treachery from those considered loyal. That's what makes this job so damned impossible."

Impossible, indeed. For didn't adversaries each pray to the same God for victory? Things were seldom black and white in life. Even this business with who should be on the throne was several shades of gray. But in the end, order must be kept or else civilization disintegrated into barbarity and savagery.

"Are you certain about Monteith?" Genuine remorse creasing Sir Walter's face as he shook his white bewigged head. "He'll be put to death, you know."

Why was he so obsessed about Monteith? Surely the list he held contained the names of many other influential people. Possibly individuals more prominent and powerful than the earl.

"Aye, I'm sure." Brushing a palm over his stubbled jaw, Camden gave a curt nod. "My betrothed heard him. Saw him hand Etherin'ton that list." He pointed at the paper. "And she kens of a secret compartment in Monteith's study. I'd vow there is more evidence within."

"Indeed." A spark of interest glinted in Sir Walter's poignant eyes as he refolded the paper. "I should very much like to see the contents. Indeed, I would." Rocking back on his heels, he grasped his lapel with one hand. "In point of fact..." His voice trailed off, the perceptiveness that made him a master at the game of subterfuge and intrigue turning his eyes flinty. "Hmm."

What?

He settled that unnerving gaze upon Camden. "How long a journey is it to Edinburgh?"

Edinburgh? Why, for God's sake?

He didn't mean to travel there *now?*

No, surely Sir Walter contemplated leaving after the men had slept.

Which meant, he'd either take Etherington with him, send Camden and Bryston to escort the blackguard to London, or entrust the traitor with his soldiers to do likewise.

The latter wasn't a good idea, and Camden wouldn't hesitate to say so. Not with a man as cunning as Etherington.

Camden rolled a shoulder, feigning disinterest. By God, the men were likely half-pished by now. "Three hours, more or less, with ideal road conditions. Faster on horseback, of course."

But Sir Walter Makepeace always traveled in a very comfortable, very cumbersome coach.

Make that four hours, at least.

With a decisive nod, he announced, "We're for Edinburgh, Kennedy. Ready your men. We'll depart at first light."

Christ.

He'd have to wake Bethea. Perhaps Sir Walter would allow him to remain behind or delay their departure for a few hours. "My betrothed—"

"About that." Lines bracketing Sir Walter's mouth and his abundant eyebrows knitted into a single line, he harrumphed. "The poor girl—ward to Roxdale, isn't she?"

"Aye." What did it matter to the adviser?

"I cannot do anything about her abduction or the difficulties she's endured," Sir Walter said, striding to the door. "But she's done the Crown a great service, and I can see the blot upon her reputation rectified to a degree."

How, precisely?

Premonition prickled the length of Camden's spine.

He detected the unspoken question in Camden's eyes.

"Come, Kennedy. You disappoint me." Sir Walter chuckled, genuine jollity lighting his eyes. "The solution is simple. You'll marry before we depart, and then we'll spread the tale that, overcome by love and impatience to wed, you eloped with your Miss Glanville."

Keane will fuckin' kill me.

EIGHT

Bethea removed Camden's wool coat and frowned at her impossibly wrinkled gown. Dirt stained the hem as well as her shoes. Giving a small shrug, she proceeded to wash her face and hands.

She was never one to fret over that which she couldn't change. Besides, it was possible the gown, as well as her shoes, could be salvaged. If not, then another less fortunate soul might make good use of them.

Examining her face in the looking glass, other than her rumpled hair and shadows of fatigue ringing her eyes, she didn't appear much worse for wear. Her head ached, but the earlier queasiness had passed. In fact, she anticipated enjoying the fragrant Scotch pie awaiting her.

Her abduction had meant she'd missed supper, and despite escaping an undeniably perilous situation, her stomach gnawed hollowly. But then the reality of her current situation seeped into her mind, and trepidation tempered her hunger.

No one need tell her she was ruined.

Inextricably and irredeemably.

Keane would likely send her packing straightaway to

Trentwick Castle, where she'd live the remainder of her days in shame and scorn. With all of those cats. Well, Keane's Scottish wildcats. Och, he *might* find a Scot willing to wed a tainted wife, but her dreams of a love-match and happily ever after had been shattered the moment Etherington clobbered her.

It wasn't bloody fair.

She'd done nothing wrong. Nothing. She refused to feel remorse for overhearing traitors plotting. And yet, because of the actions of those reprehensible blackguards, her life and her future had been inalterably changed. And not for the better.

More exasperating was the knowledge that if she were a man, her virtue would be a non-issue.

Fighting tears—all the more infuriating because she wasn't given to crying at the drop of a feather—she removed the remaining pins from her hair. She combed her fingers through the length to remove the majority of the snarls, taking care not to aggravate the knot at the back of her head. After plaiting the waist-length tresses, she searched for something to tie the ends together.

A piece of lace hung loose on her sleeve, and she gave it a vicious tug, taking her frustration out on the poor garment. Once Bethea had tied her hair, she inhaled a bracing breath.

No sense in moping about, sullen and petulant.

What was done was done.

Good had come of this debacle—apprehending Etherington, and soon, hopefully, Monteith as well. Which meant she no longer had to endure his foul attention.

Perhaps, after a time, Keane would permit her to travel and take Branwen with her, for the disgrace would taint her dear sister as well. He might even hire a companion to accompany her.

After all, Bethea was of age. But—and that was a very big

but—she had no funds of her own. Mayhap he could be persuaded to give her the dowry he'd settled upon her?

Feeling marginally mollified with that notion but still heartsick about the disgrace her disappearance would inevitably cause her family, she set to her delicious Scotch pie, washing it down with wonderfully strong, if a trifle tepid, tea.

Despite her determination to stay awake, her eyelids kept drifting downward. A boisterous laugh from the courtyard or the common room jolted her awake more than once before she gave in to her exhaustion.

After covering herself with the extra quilt from the foot of the bed, she sank into the rather lumpy straw mattress and even lumpier pillow. Never had a bed felt half so comfortable.

Sleep beckoned, and, still pondering if Keane might be amenable to the possibility of her escaping the humiliation by traveling for six months or a year, she yawned.

I've always wanted to visit Rome. The Pantheon and the Colosseum. The Roman Forum—

Sleep claimed her, bringing blessed forgetfulness.

Knock. Knock. Knock.

Struggling awake, Bethea crinkled her brow. Who banged at her bedchamber door in the middle of the night?

Knock. Knock. Knock.

"Bethea?"

Knock. Knock.

A man?

Not Keane.

Forcing her eyelids open, she stared around her in confusion.

Where was she?

"Bethea?" *Knock. Knock.* "'Tis Camden." *Knock. Knock.* "Open the door. 'Tis important."

"Camden?'" she murmured groggily.

What?

Memory flooded back, slamming into her with the impact of a pair of millstones.

Och, God.

She scrambled off the bed and hurriedly lifted the board barring the entrance.

At once, he shoved the door open and slipped inside. His presence seemed to fill the space and suck the very air from the tiny chamber.

Pushing her hair off her face, she met his tense gaze. "Did it no' go well with Etherin'ton?"

Something had him in a temper. Every plane of his face stood out starkly, and a grim line pulled his full mouth into a stern ribbon.

"Camden?" Frissons of alarm skittered down her back and tangled low in her belly. She placed a hand on his forearm.

He stiffened, the muscle beneath her palm twitching. Even as he did so, his warmth penetrated her skin and his masculine scent met her nostrils: fresh sweat, leather, horse, and another woodsy aroma.

"Bethea?" He summoned what was, at best, a tenuous smile.

She stepped away, tilting her chin to see him better.

He was, after all, three or four inches over six feet tall, and while she was no short lass at six inches over five feet herself, he towered over her. The immense width of his shoulders and chest, the corded column of his neck, and the tree-trunks he had for thighs all contributed to the impression of him as a powerful, brawny warrior.

The fierce scowl darkening his face at the moment did as well.

Why was he so upset? How long had he been below?

It must be near dawn. She cast a glance at the shuttered window. No hint of light peeked through any of the cracks, but if the sky were still obstructed by heavy cloud cover, daylight would creep upon the inn like a low blanket of fog upon a loch.

"I assume somethin' happened to disgruntle ye," she offered, prying gently. She wasn't one to poke her nose in another's private affairs, but whatever had Camden disgruntled pertained to her, or else he wouldn't be in this chamber with her.

"Aye, lass." He puffed out a breath, the motion emphasizing the breadth of his sculpted chest, as he shoved a hand through his thick, black hair. "A wee bit of a problem has arisen."

Bethea would wager whatever had him discomposed was more than a *wee* problem. Despite her impatience, she bridled her tongue and waited for him to say whatever it was he needed to say.

Planting his hands on his lean hips—not that she noticed men's hips or the very apparent bulge at his loins—he took a long, leisurely look over her form. An almost possessive glint entered his clear blue eyes, framed by sinfully thick lashes.

Even *her* lashes weren't that thick. And the way he looked at her just now... Well, any woman would take exception to that masculine appraisal.

What yer feelin' is nae offense.

Crossing her arms, she narrowed her gaze in reproach. "Enjoyin' yerself?"

He grinned, a cocky, self-confident smirk that made her

simultaneously long to slap the smugness off his face and also kiss that molded mouth.

What was wrong with her?

"Aye." A seductive wink followed his keen assessment. "Ye are verra lovely. I've always thought so."

He had?

Despite the inappropriateness of his perusal, heat like warm custard or honey suffused her. Mustering supreme effort, she subdued her feminine response to him. Arms still crossed, she canted her head and arched a starchy eyebrow upward. "*Well*?"

His mirth evaporated, and solemnness transformed the contours of his face.

Something *was* amiss.

"I told ye that I had to claim ye were my betrothed to keep ye safe from—" He stepped nearer and took one of her hands in his rough one. "Well, ye ken what from."

Violation. Rape. Despoilment. Being set upon.

There were a number of polite ways to describe being taken by force.

Keane was the product of rape, and he'd never shied away from warning Bethea and Branwen of the way men might attempt to abuse them. Not that he'd permitted men near enough very often for such a thing to occur.

She didn't blame or resent Camden for claiming they were betrothed. He'd said what he must to keep her from a horrible fate. So why did he look so discomfited now, as if he struggled to speak what was on his mind?

"Aye. I ken, and I appreciate ye did what ye must. I'm no' angry if that is what has ye worried." Mesmerized, she watched him brush his big thumb back and forth across the back of her hand. The movement was at once soothing and sensual. Much like the deep, melodious baritone of his voice.

He remained silent, so she tried again. "I understand, ye had nae choice, Camden. Dinna fash yerself about it."

His eyes had deepened to indigo, and the teasing glint he normally regarded her with was absent. So very serious. Whatever could have ever-cheerful Camden Kennedy this somber?

Odd that he should be so concerned over the matter.

Perhaps Bethea had misread his interest in her at Trentwick, and he was truly opposed to anyone believing them betrothed.

Her heart gave a queer twinge at the thought, though why it should, she couldn't imagine. Wasn't she the one who wanted a chance to meet other men?

"I promise, I'll nae hold ye to the fabrication." In an attempt to lighten the heavy mood in the room, she grinned and winked. "I'll nae be exchangin' vows with ye. Ye willna find yerself saddled with an unwanted wife."

He brought his vivid blue gaze up to meet hers, and his eyes probed the depths of her soul. Something unnamable flickered behind the cage that was her ribs. It was as if he tried silently to communicate with her. As if he couldn't summon the right words.

That had never been an issue with him before. He'd always had a glib reply, a flirtatious comment, or a cheeky retort.

He touched her cheek with a bent knuckle, and she widened her eyes, taken aback at the affectionate gesture.

"Aye lass. Ye will. Below. In ten minutes."

What?

"Pardon?" Bethea's mouth went dry, and her heart seized mid-beat. Then, feeling like an utter fool, she realized he but jested. "That's no' verra funny, Camden. I about lost ten years—"

"I'm nae jestin', lass." From the pained expression on his

face and harshness of his deep burr, it seemed he very much wished he were. "A high-rankin' advisor to His Majesty, Sir Walter Makepeace, has decreed that we will wed before returnin' to Edinburgh at first light."

"But... But...that's ridiculous." She shook her head, withdrawing her hand and backing away. "Ye dinna have any desire to marry me, and I dinna want to wed ye."

"Och, and ye can read my mind?" His expression grew impossibly sterner, his tone dangerous.

Odin's teeth, had she offended him?

Most men she knew would rejoice at escaping forced nuptials.

"I didna mean that as an insult, Camden. I only meant I wouldna hold ye to the vow ye made to protect me. What kind of a woman do ye think I am?"

She moved toward the door, but he caught her arm, his huge hand almost encircling her wrist.

"Let me speak to Sir Walter and explain the situation," she insisted.

He shook his head, his hair brushing his shoulders with the movement. "Nae, lass. If ye tell him we arena betrothed in truth, I dinna ken if Bryston and I can protect ye. The men have been drinkin' and are—ah—"

Bright color blotched his prominent cheekbones, and she almost giggled at the incongruity. This burly Highlander—a bit of a rogue himself—blushing at the mention of fornication?

"They require female *companionship* because Mrs. Dowerdy runs a *respectable* establishment?" She mimicked the innkeeper's admonishing tenor.

"Aye." He crooked his mouth sideways. "That's one way of puttin' it."

"I'll tell him I canna possibly marry without my family

present." Again, she moved toward the door. "That ought to satisfy him."

He blocked her path and trapped her by gently placing his palms upon her shoulders. "Nae, lass. He's determined to salvage yer reputation and insists we wed immediately. I've argued with him for the past hour. He's resolute, and he has the ear of His Majesty. We dinna have a choice."

"Poppycock," she snorted. "Of course, we do. Your Sir Walter canna force us to marry."

Could he?

She stitched her eyebrows together as she squinted at Camden's too-wide chest. His shirt was unlaced several inches, and tantalizing curly, black hair peeked at her.

Oh, she wanted to slide her fingers through that thick mat. Bury her nose in that hair too.

What was she thinking?

He'd just announced a Sir Walter Makepeace demanded they marry—*now*—and she was indulging in decadent thoughts about his chest hair?

Addled. Aye, off my head.

The blow *had* damaged her reasoning.

Giving herself a mental shake and a severe admonishment for noticing his deliciously hairy chest, Bethea refocused on the matter at hand.

"Who, exactly, is this Sir Walter Makepeace?" She'd never heard of the man, but that was no surprise.

"He's an advisor to the king. A delegate with the power and authority to act on the king's behalf."

She narrowed her eyes. She didn't care if Sir Walter Makepeace was the bloody king himself. No one was going to trap her into a marriage of convenience.

Camden placed a bent finger beneath her chin and levered

her gaze up to meet his. Compassion and something considerably warmer shone in his eyes. "We will marry, lass."

His tone brooked no argument, and in that interminable instant, she knew it for the truth it was. Neither of them had any choice. She wasn't sure what this man's power was over Camden, but he'd conceded defeat regarding their union.

Marriage *would* salvage her reputation. Her reputation for her dreams—to choose her husband and marry for love. More irony.

"Nae." She shook her head. "Nae," she whispered again.

Mother of God, she'd not considered this. Ruination and banishment, aye. A forced marriage wasn't fair to Camden either.

"'Tis nae fair," she choked out, furious at the moisture blurring her vision. "Ye were bein' a gentleman. I dinna think even Keane would expect it of ye."

Would he?

In truth, he might. And Bethea felt more the fool for not having considered that too.

A tear trickled from the corner of her eye, but before she could angrily swipe it away, Camden caught it with a bent finger.

"I'm sorry, lass. I didna think ye'd be so opposed to the match."

"'Tis no' *ye* I'm opposed to, but a marriage of convenience," she murmured. Merely ruined, she might find love someday. As a married woman, there wasn't a chance in hell of that.

He drew her against his chest, and she wrapped her arms around him, burying her face into his manliness.

"I suppose, after a time, we can seek an annulment or a divorce," he said. "I'll nae take ye to my bed." A hint of regret colored his avowal, and the timbre of his voice stalled her heart for a pair of beats. "But for now, we must exchange vows."

She angled her head up to look at him, seeing the earnestness in his eyes. The consternation and remorse there too. Those penetrating eyes sank to her parted mouth, and then, with a muffled groan, he kissed her.

Slowly. Gently. A wonderfully soft, warm caress.

And she realized she'd yearned for his mouth on hers for weeks. Since she'd danced with him that first night of the Hogmanay celebration. How could she have been so blind that she'd not seen what was before her?

She felt something for Camden. Something intense and heady.

Standing on her toes, she twined her arms around his sturdy neck, reveling in the maelstrom swirling inside her.

Bethea gasped in pleasant surprise at the tingles humming through her body and the splendidness of pressing her breasts and torso against his hard contours. She wanted to crawl inside Camden, to explore every glorious, firm curve and masculine angle.

His tongue teased the seam of her mouth, and she opened for him, allowing him access to that which no man had explored before. He made a low, gravelly sound in his throat; one hand splayed between her shoulders and the other grazed her hip.

Through the layers of her gown and petticoats, her skin grew hot, a peculiar yearning building deep in her belly.

A single, sharp rap on the door interrupted their kiss.

"Camden, the reverend has arrived," Bryston McPherson called softly through the slightly lopsided door. "Sir Walter wants ye and yer—*ah*—betrothed below."

Breathing irregularly, Bethea attempted to regain her

composure. She'd never dreamed a kiss could rattle her senses so thoroughly.

But that hadn't been *just* a kiss.

That had been an introduction to passion. Passion that, until this moment, she hadn't realized burned hotly beneath her proper exterior. And she couldn't help but wonder what it would be like to be Camden Kennedy's wife in every way. To take him to her bed and let him do with her what he would. To do with *him* what *she* would.

"Aye. We'll be down momentarily." Camden rested his forehead against hers, the tenderness and consideration making her want to weep. "It will be all right, Bethea. I vow to ye."

She couldn't fathom how, but inexplicably, she trusted him, even in this impossible situation.

"All right," she finally agreed.

Not an overly exuberant acceptance to a proposal. But then, Camden hadn't proposed, had he? She'd never met this Sir Walter Makepeace, but she couldn't like anyone who lorded their power over another.

With a reassuring smile, Camden tucked her hand into his arm and led her below. He lent her his strength as they spoke their vows, giving her hand a comforting squeeze every few minutes.

The tired-looking cleric barely hid his yawns as he droned on, blinking sleepily. Behind him, Sir Walter Makepeace beamed as if Camden were his son and he'd granted him a knighthood.

And then it was over.

And, God and all the saints and angels help her, she was Mrs. Camden Kennedy.

Knocked on the head, abducted, and married.

All because she'd wanted to spare Branwen humiliation.

Camden gave Bethea a chaste kiss on the cheek before shaking Sir Walter's extended hand, and then Bryston McPherson's as he slapped Camden's back.

"Congratulations, my friend," Bryston said.

Camden merely cocked a superior brow and leveled his friend a quelling look.

Grinning, McPherson gave her a kindly wink and a nod. "*Mrs. Kennedy.*"

She'd have to have been deaf not to hear the humor in his words.

Did he think this a grand jest?

People's lives had been manipulated, possibly ruined.

"I hope we'll have the pleasure of wishin' ye well soon, Mr. McPherson," she said with false sweetness. It would serve him right to find himself leg-shackled through no fault of his own.

Shaking his blond head, the earring in his left ear swinging with the motion, he chuckled and threw up both hands. "Never say it."

"We'll see," Camden muttered beneath his breath.

Twenty minutes later, Beatha sat in Etherington's coach once more, her new husband sitting across from her, as they jostled and bounced their way to Edinburgh.

The headache that had niggled earlier thrummed full on now. With two fingers from each hand, Bethea rubbed her temples in a slow, circular motion.

What in God's name have I done?

NINE

Easter Road outside Edinburgh
22 March 1721

Camden had insisted that he and Bethea take this coach, rather than sharing Sir Walter's. He well knew his superior would've preferred Camden travel with him, but by damn, he wasn't abandoning his new wife minutes after saying, "I do."

Instead, he'd made arrangements to meet Sir Walter after seeing Bethea safely to the bosom of her family. The man could hardly argue the point, as he'd been the one to insist on the nuptials. Besides, he'd agreed Roxdale was entitled to an explanation.

"Yes, yes, indeed. You are quite right, Camden," he'd said, shrugging on his black, satin-lined cloak. "See to your lovely bride, soothe any qualms her family may have, and meet me at Monteith's at, let's say, three?" He crooked a grizzled eyebrow as he hooked the clasp at his throat. "Is that sufficient time to set things to right?"

Nae. It would take months. Years even.

Sir Walter didn't know Keane or Bethea. Exchanging vows

had been the easy part. It was everything that came after—none of which had been anticipated or planned—that would be an unholy mess to untangle.

"Aye, that should suffice," he acquiesced.

Now, three hours later, he held his new wife in his arms as she slept the sleep of the utterly exhausted. At least she'd been spared a sick stomach by sleeping most of the journey.

Bethea had said little the first few miles, her thoughts obviously elsewhere, until her lids had drifted downward and she'd fallen asleep. She also suffered from a headache, though she didn't whisper so much as one word in complaint.

Slumber had eluded him, but he'd drawn her into his arms and held her, feeling a protectiveness and—something else. Something foreign but enticing suffusing him.

His lack of rancor and frustration at the situation astonished him. Yes, Camden took orders and carried them out with precision and expertise, but he'd never been a man who'd permitted himself to be manipulated.

Bethea's dark lashes fanned her porcelain cheeks, and her pink rosebud mouth parted as she slumbered. Wrapped in a servant's brown cloak they'd purchased from one of the barmaids for twice what it was worth, her subtle perfume wafted to him now and again.

Lilacs befit her. Fresh and sweet, but with a hint of something alluring as well.

Camden had always faced the truth squarely, and he'd do the same in these circumstances. If he were entirely honest with himself, he hadn't been averse to marrying Bethea. How they came to be husband and wife wasn't the most romantic or ideal progression, but he could, in all honesty, say he didn't mind.

She, on the other hand, had been utterly appalled. Only

Camden's assurance that the union could be voided later had led her to concede to go through with the ceremony.

The woman sleeping in his arms had fascinated him since he'd first seen her at Eytone Hall's *cèilidh* celebration last August. She'd also intrigued and delighted him with her quick wit, a ready smile, and perpetual kindness to all during the week-long Hogmanay celebration at Trentwick Castle.

And yet, he hadn't permitted his interest to go beyond a mild flirtation, firmly believing he wasn't free to wed. Men in his line of work put their lives in peril regularly. Now, however, he found himself with a very alluring but reluctant wife. And the truth was, he didn't object to the union nearly as much as he ought to have.

Didn't object to holding her in his arms or the possibility of exploring her very alluring curves. What would it be like to fall asleep with her in his embrace every night? Awaken her with a kiss each morn?

If it had been any other woman, he'd have refused Sir Walter. And that epiphany both disturbed and stunned him.

The timing was atrocious, as were the circumstances. But marriage to Bethea Glanville—nae, that wasn't unpleasant at all.

There was something powerful and enigmatic between him and Bethea.

It might only be a physical attraction, but Camden didn't think so. He'd slated his carnal desires with willing women for over a decade and had never felt this internal pull. And that made it all the more important that he not succumb to the unfamiliar emotion swirling around inside him.

It was one thing to seek an annulment or divorce for an unwanted marriage, but it would be something else entirely if he came to love Bethea. Hell, he suspected he was halfway there already. He'd never want to let her go if he allowed his feelings free rein. But neither would he make her stay if she truly wanted to leave.

He exhaled a long breath. It was too soon for those disheartening thoughts in any event.

In order for her reputation to sustain the least amount of damage, people must believe they'd eloped. Then in a few months or a year, they could proceed with the annulment, though that would bring a degree of ignominy as well.

He suspected Bethea wouldn't care about dispersions directed at her, but she would about her sister. She was fiercely loyal and devoted to those she loved. She'd not want to taint Branwen's chances of a brilliant match, and in fact, might want to delay the dissolution of the marriage until her sister had wed.

Running a finger over Bethea's plump lower lip, he closed his eyes.

Camden hadn't meant to kiss her at The Boar and Brew. It had just happened, and he couldn't regret it. He could still taste her sweetness. A fire smoldered within Bethea Glanville —Kennedy—and he longed to be the man to fan those passionate embers into a blazing conflagration.

Opening his eyes, he gazed down upon her. She settled closer to him, her eyelids moving as she dreamed and a little snore escaping her.

He grinned, utterly entranced.

Odin's bones, this delectable woman was his wife. *His wife.*

How in hell was he going to keep his hands off her?

Even now, desire surged through him, and his cock grew hard beneath her.

As surely as heather bloomed in the Highlands, they'd share his chamber at Eytone Hall. After all, why would two people so in love that they'd toddled off to exchange vows over the anvil keep separate rooms?

Perhaps he could persuade Berget, his brother Graeme's bride of only a few months, to move them to a bigger chamber at least. One with a dressing room attached.

Aye, that might do.

He could sleep in there, but he'd have to take care the servants didn't learn of it.

Shite, who was he trying to fool? Servants knew *everything.*

He'd think of something. Maybe he'd request another assignment immediately.

Except, he didn't want Bethea to feel he'd deserted her. She'd struggled enough about their forced marriage. If he took off at once, wouldn't she feel abandoned and betrayed?

Permitting his eyelids to drift closed again, he pondered Sir Walter's decision to assign Bryston the task of seeing a petulant Etherington to London. Accompanied by six soldiers, Bryston had given a cocky salute, and his mouth quirked into an even cockier grin when he had promised to contact Camden the instant he returned to Scotland.

The six mercenaries had received their pay and bonus and had been summarily discharged. None, save Anderson, grumbled overly much. They'd appreciated the relatively easy work and generous payments.

However, as Etherington was in custody and Monteith soon would be, their services were no longer required. In truth, Camden had never trusted the scurvy lot.

Bryston still didn't know the whole of the tale about Camden and Bethea's false betrothal and their very real marriage. Camden hadn't missed the hilarity in Bryston's eyes and voice either. He thought fate had trapped Camden. Little did Bryston know how willingly Camden had walked into the snare.

Camden quite looked forward to calling on the Earl of Monteith. And perhaps, breaking the assling's nose or rendering him a eunuch over what he'd intended for Bethea.

For her part, she'd explained precisely which volumes to remove to reveal the hidden compartment. Camden was confident they'd have no trouble finding it.

What he wasn't confident about was Keane's reception in a few minutes.

They neared Bethea's home, and he gently shook her awake. "Bethea, darlin', we're almost there."

She stirred and slowly opened her eyes, blinking up at him. Still drowsy, her quicksilver gaze was soft and slightly confused. He knew the moment she remembered all that had occurred, and she swiftly sat up.

"Did I truly sleep the entire journey?" she asked groggily as she smoothed her palms over her hair.

"Aye. Ye were exhausted." He tucked a silky tress behind her ear. "How is yer headache?"

"Och, 'tis gone." Glancing out the window, she sucked her lower lip into her mouth and clamped down with her neat upper teeth. "I dinna ken what to expect." She sent him a sideways glance. "When they find out we're married..."

When Keane found out, she meant.

A flush pinkened her cheeks, but she didn't look away.

"I'll be right there with ye. I dinna see how anyone can object when they ken the circumstances." He hoped to God that was true.

Keane might not see it that way.

Eyes wide and uncertain, Bethea gave a small nod.

He despised seeing this vivacious woman trepidatious about facing her family.

"I willna allow Keane to bully ye." She drew in a shuddery

breath as she toyed with the pleats of the cloak. "He only means well."

His heart turned over at her attempt to hearten him.

"I ken, lass." Camden did know, but when Keane had taken on the responsibility of two wards, he also vowed to keep them from harm. Quite likely, he'd see Bethea's abduction as a failure on his part. "He's a reasonable man. He'll understand," Camden assured her, not altogether certain that was the truth.

"Aye, but this is rather a unique situation." She sighed and smoothed the rough cloak over her gown. "I blame myself. I never should've ventured into that room. All of this—" She swept her hand between them. "My abduction, our hasty marriage, would've been avoided had I no' been where I shouldna have been."

"Mayhap. But then we'd no' ken about Monteith's treachery or the hidden compartment." He winked and pressed a kiss to her forehead before rolling his shoulder. "Ye'd make a verra good agent."

Something akin to pride erased the worry from her eyes.

The clock hadn't yet chimed twelve when Etherington's coach groaned to a stop outside a fashionable house on the city's outskirts. Parkhill Hall, Bethea had called Keane's house in Edinburgh. The acrid smoke that perpetually hovered over the city, staining the buildings and often burning one's eyes, was only slightly less thick here.

"Ready, Bethea?"

She swallowed then, searching his gaze with hers, and nodded. "As ready as I'll ever be, I suppose."

Camden disembarked the coach first, and Bethea had only stepped from the conveyance when Roxdale's front door flew open.

In less than two heartbeats, Keane and Marjorie sprinted

down the four stairs. Behind them, using a cane to support herself, Branwen hobbled laboriously to the entrance. At least a half dozen servants had also crowded onto the stairway and in the entry.

Tears ran down Branwen's face as she held a fist to her mouth.

Upon seeing her sister's distress, Bethea's eyes filled with moisture.

"Bethea, darling." Marjorie enfolded her in a tight embrace. "I'm so very, very relieved that you are safe." The gaze she turned on Camden held inquisitiveness but no condemnation.

The same could not be said of Keane. He glared predatory daggers at Camden, his seething fury barely in check. "I'm *sure* ye have a damn good explanation."

"Aye," Camden concurred, rather too nonchalant. "A *damn* good one, indeed."

Bethea untangled herself from Marjorie's embrace, but before she could defend Camden or explain, Keane wrapped his arms around her in a fierce hug.

"Lass, I aged twenty years since last night. Thank God, ye're safe."

Over her midnight hair, he sent Camden a wordless message.

She had bloody well better be all right.

"Bethea," Branwen called in a tear-clogged voice as she tried to descend the stairs on her injured feet.

Bethea dashed to her and enfolded her in her embrace. "Darlin', ye shouldna be puttin' weight on yer foot."

"Pshaw. What flimflam. My bruised feet are nothin'." She burst into tears and flung her arms around Bethea. "I... I was so afraid I'd lost ye."

Marjorie gave a pointed glance at the street. Several

passersby openly gawked, and more than one intrigued face pressed against the window of a neighboring house. "Let's go inside, shall we?"

"Yes," Bethea agreed, wrapping an arm about her sister's waist. At the top of the stairs, she paused to cast a glance over her shoulder. Worry pleated her usually smooth forehead as she swung her attention from Camden to Keane and back to him again.

Camden swept his mouth into his most disarming smile, and she offered the slightest upward tilt of her mouth in response. Sweet lass, she continued to fret about Keane's reaction. Surely, he wouldn't punch Camden in public.

He hoped.

With a final, troubled glance at Keane, she helped her sister inside.

Camden started forward, but Keane's firm hand on his forearm stopped him. "If ye have touched her—"

"Relax, cousin. All is well. I married her." He'd never know what devil prompted him to blurt *that,* but it felt damn good to say it.

Keane's jaw came unhinged, and then his mouth worked, but nothing but angry rasps came forth. "Ye..." He finally managed, his gruff voice as rough as a gravel lane. "Ye *married* her?"

"Aye. I wed the lass to preserve her reputation after saving her from an abduction." Camden grinned and slapped his flummoxed cousin on the back. "Ye can thank me inside."

TEN

Parkhill Hall
Edinburgh, Scotland
Late Morning
22 March 1721

Relieved of her borrowed cloak and settled onto a plush brocade striped chaise in the green salon, Marjorie and Branwen on either side of her, Bethea looked to Camden.

Would he announce their *news*, or should she?

Keane paced back and forth, his hair unkempt and dark stubble covering his jaw. Face ruddy and black eyebrows slashed into a stern line, he seemed incapable of speech. Well, of polite speech, that was.

Wrath radiated off him in thick, tense waves, and every few steps, he fired Camden murderous glowers that would have smote a lesser man into cinders.

Marjorie observed her husband, a fretful frown puckering her forehead.

He knows. Keane knows *Camden and I are married.*

Bethea narrowed her gaze and cut Camden a reproachful look. Skewing a rather starchy eyebrow, she mouthed, "*Well?*"

He cleared his throat and clasped his hands behind his back. "As I've already told my cousin, circumstances required Bethea and me to marry this morn."

Branwen gasped, the color draining from her face as she grasped about clumsily, searching for Bethea's hand to clutch in hers.

"Marry? You're married?" Marjorie said, her shock apparent but subdued. She was never one to overreact without an explanation, but even *she* looked utterly confounded. "Please, do explain."

Concern filling her brown eyes, she followed Keane's rigidly controlled movements with her gaze.

"Aye, do." Thunder reverberated in her husband's voice, and lightning sparked in his eyes.

Bethea feared he was on the verge of apoplexy, and her mind raced for a way to diffuse the volatile tension that was thick enough to slice with a saber.

"It began when I took Branwen to the ladies' retirin' room." Bethea quickly recounted the events, only leaving out the kiss she and Camden had shared. Not only was that too private, but it was also sure to rile Keane further. And there'd be no annulment should that tidbit become public knowledge.

Standing before the fireplace, one hand on his hip and the other cradling his nape, Keane stared hard at her and then Camden. "God damn that bastard. I'll strangle Monteith with my bare hands," he bit out through clenched teeth.

"Keane," Marjorie softly admonished, the understanding in her eyes softening her reproach. "The girls."

Bethea and Branwen exchanged a knowing glance. They

were hardly girls, and they'd heard much worse in the great hall, stable, and bailey.

Speaking of girls, however, where were Cora and Elana, Marjorie's pixyish red-haired daughters? Probably sequestered in their chamber, lest things become heated between their beloved Uncle Camden and equally adored stepfather.

"*Leannan.*" *Sweetheart.* Keane heaved a weighty sigh, aggravation and frustration alternating across his countenance. "Even ye must concede this is a bloody mess. Surely everyone at the ball kens of Bethea's disappearance."

Bethea winced inwardly, a hint of despair cresting in her chest. She'd naively hoped the incident had been kept quiet. Or that only a select, critical few were aware she'd vanished.

"I canna be sure, of course," Camden said. "But from my conversation with Etherin'ton, I've concluded Monteith intended to swoop in and play the hero by rescuin' her from him." His expression and voice turned flinty. "Then, the bugger intended to ruin her to force her to wed him."

"As if I ever would." Revulsion caused Bethea to shudder, and Marjorie patted her arm in commiseration. "I'd rather die than marry that doughy, putrid pizzle."

"*Pizzle?*" Branwen asked, struggling unsuccessfully to subdue the twitching of her mouth.

Marjorie choked on a laugh and swiftly pretended to cough behind her hand.

Keane opened and closed his mouth, no doubt wondering how in the hell Bethea even knew the word and likely praying she didn't know its meaning.

She did, indeed.

The Roma that traveled through the Highlands every spring were responsible. She'd learned a few other expressions from them too. The gypsies were a flamboyant, spirited people who, unlike High Society, didn't put on airs or speak out of two sides of their mouths. However, they could also be cunning and crafty and most definitely colorful in their speech. Hence *pizzle* for penis.

Camden did not attempt to hide the upward slant of his mouth at her choice of words. He pulled at his ear lobe, his gaze working over her, a shadow of possessiveness there. "The point is rather moot now, as ye are married to me."

Awareness swept Bethea, and this time when a shiver tiptoed the length of her spine, aversion didn't cause it.

"Are ye truly wed?" Branwen whispered in Bethea's ear, equal parts fascination and astonishment in her tone.

"Aye, but in name only," she whispered back under cover of the rather intense exchange commencing between Keane, Camden, and Marjorie. "We had nae choice."

"What will ye do?" Branwen asked, worry darkening her eyes to the shade of the sky before a winter tempest.

Hitching a shoulder, Bethea meshed her lips together. "An annulment after a respectable amount of time has passed to put rumors to rest." She darted Camden a glance beneath her lashes. "Or a divorce if we canna acquire an annulment."

"Oh." Something in Branwen's voice made Bethea give her a searching look. "And... in the meanwhile?"

Aye, that was the two-ton question. One she and Camden hadn't discussed. One she wasn't sure she wanted to.

Would Bethea move to Eytone Hall or Camden to Trentwick Castle? Or would they live elsewhere? Or—would they live apart? The latter wouldn't reinforce the wildly in love ruse, but it would make obtaining an annulment easier if they never resided together.

Surely Camden's assignments would require him to be absent, perhaps for weeks on end. Just how dangerous were his missions? A chill slithered down her spine, dual venoms of apprehension and worry coiling around her belly.

She didn't like the idea of him being in danger or taking risks. Even if it were for King and country. But some men thrived on intrigue and peril. Her father, a reckless sea captain, had. And his last madcap escapade had taken his and Mama's lives.

Was Camden one of those men? One always looking for the next adventure?

Firming her mouth, Bethea searched the archives of her mind. She knew so little about the man she now called husband. Other than he kissed divinely, and there was much more to Camden than the accomplished flirt and rapscallion he presented to the world.

She'd never have suspected him of being an agent for the Crown.

And dinna forget, a confessed marauder and part-time highwayman.

Although supposedly *those* were guises.

What other secrets did Camden Kennedy have?

Did she really want to know?

"'Tis settled then," Keane said, though no satisfaction lit his eyes, and no happiness softened his features.

His no-nonsense statement effectively ended Bethea's woolgathering.

What was settled?

She looked between Keane and Camden, searching for a hint of what she'd missed.

His expression grim, Camden gave a terse nod. "I'd like a word with Bethea before I leave."

Ah, his meeting with Sir Walter. He'd need to depart soon.

A glance at the ormolu and marble clock atop the fireplace revealed he had plenty of time.

"Of course," Marjorie agreed as she rose. Smiling broadly, she gave him an exuberant hug. "I cannot say I'm not thrilled that two of my favorite people are now husband and wife. 'Tis another way our clans are united."

Her eyes grew misty with emotion, and she blinked rapidly.

"Aye, Marjorie." Camden gave her an affectionate peck on the cheek. "Should I call ye mum now?" Considering he was a year older than she, the question proved ludicrous, but it had the desired effect of defusing a degree of tension.

She laughed, and even Keane's mouth tipped upward.

Still baffled about what she'd missed, Bethea returned Branwen's embrace.

"I'll see ye upstairs in a few minutes," Branwen said. "I'll start packin' yer belongin's."

So Bethea *was* to leave then. Bundled off like a wayward child. She couldn't help the spark of resentment that flamed behind her breastbone.

Until she reminded herself it was unfair to jump to that conclusion when she'd not heard the conversation.

Drat her inattentiveness and daydreaming.

With Marjorie's help, Branwen limped from the salon, Keane trailing behind them.

At the door, his hand on the latch, he turned and offered his first genuine smile. "Camden, I do appreciate what ye did for Bethea. I ken yer hands were tied."

"Ye'd have done the same, Cousin." Camden acknowledged the thanks with a wry smile and inclination of his dark head.

"Aye." Keane's gaze slid to Bethea. "I'll await ye in the entry."

After he'd quit the room, Camden settled his large form on the chaise beside Bethea. Why did the room suddenly feel tiny and as if the air had been sucked out of it? And why must she be so aware of the virile male so close that his heat beckoned her nearer? His musky, masculine scent enticed her—drew her ever nearer, much like the proverbial moth to a flame. And yet...having her wings singed might be worth it.

"Keane's goin' with ye to arrest Monteith?" She wasn't surprised, nor particularly worried. Keane and Camden knew their way around a sword and were seasoned warriors.

"Aye. He needs to feel like he's doin' somethin' to vindicate ye." He flicked the tip of her disheveled braid. "I canna permit him to kill the rotter though. Monteith's too valuable alive."

"Mmm." Despite the truth of his words, Bethea was shocked at the degree of loathing for Monteith heating her blood. She wanted him dead. That knowledge forced her to face a side of herself that, until today, she'd never have believed existed. She was capable of deep, abiding hatred.

It made her sick to her stomach.

Camden quirked his mouth into a smile and brushed a lock of hair off her face. "I dinna ken how long this business with Monteith will take, but Keane is eager for ye and me to depart Edinburgh as soon as 'tis completed." He hesitated and then took her hand in his. "He'll spread the word that we eloped and are now enjoyin' a romantic weddin' trip."

She raised a skeptical eyebrow. "Just like that?"

"Our families are close, and we've been in love for years." His brogue deepened, and a decidedly primal glint gleamed in his blue eyes.

She nodded, having a hard time concentrating when he kept brushing his thumb over the back of her hand, and with his marble-like thigh pressing into hers. She gave a toss of her head. "Elopements are so common in Scotland. The gossip should be minimal."

Minimal?

Nae, but perhaps subdued?

His expression thoughtful, he nodded. "Unless Monteith flaps his mouth, which is doubtful given his culpability. And when he's arrested in a couple of hours, nae one will regard anythin' he says."

At the mention of Monteith, her stomach toppled over. A fake marriage was far preferable to despoilment at the earl's hands. She owed Camden much. "I'm afraid I was speakin' with Branwen and missed whatever decision ye and Keane settled on."

Since whatever they'd decided also affected her, it would've been nice to have been included in the decision. But men were forever making decisions on women's behalf, and women were expected to accept those choices docilely.

She wasn't peeved, exactly, for she recognized that if she'd been paying attention to the conversation, she might've interjected her opinion. It was unfair to blame them.

He scratched a hawkish eyebrow, a slightly enigmatic smile curving his mouth. "Yer family will remain in Edinburgh for at least a month to reinforce the elopement subterfuge, and we will journey to Culloden."

"Culloden?" She tilted her head, pulling her eyebrows together in her confusion. "No' Trentwick Castle or Eytone Hall? I dinna understand."

"Keane has a house there. Actually, more of a huntin' lodge a couple of miles outside of the township." He relaxed against the back of the chaise, drawing her with him.

She should protest but couldn't bring herself to voice an objection. In truth, it felt rather wonderful tucked into Camden's side, his heat warming her.

"We've agreed that until Monteith, Etherin'ton, and whoever else they're collaboratin' with are securely locked in whatever prison His Majesty decides upon, ye may no' be safe," he murmured into her hair.

Did he just sniff her hair?

"That's ridiculous." She snorted and shook her head, bumping his chin. She almost giggled at his grunt of pain. Instead, she focused on the absurdity of their reasoning. "Even now Bryston is takin' Etherin'ton to London, and by this afternoon, ye'll have Monteith in custody as well."

Did he know something he wasn't telling her?

"'Tis wise to never underestimate the enemy, my sweet."

He still held her hand, and she had no desire to remove it —especially when he called her his sweet.

"I understand leavin' Edinburgh," she said. "Especially if Keane says we're on a weddin' trip. But canna we go home?"

"Nae. No' for now." His expression grew serious. "We'll have to discuss where we are to live until..." Rolling a shoulder, he said, "Och, until we decide what path our futures will take."

"I take it ye didna mention the annulment to Keane.'

Camden slowly grazed his big, rough fingers along her jawline.

Bethea's breath caught on a half-sigh, half-gasp as desire, unexpected and undeniable, jolted her.

He really must stop doing that. His touch proved terribly —*deliciously*—distracting. It made her want more, want to explore whatever *this* was between them. And that was perilous because once they tripped down that convoluted road of passion and desire, there could never be any turning back.

They would remain man and wife for the rest of their lives.

Camden might want her in the way a man did a woman, and he'd certainly raised her interest in the forbidden subject, but neither had entered the arrangement willingly. And both had done so with the expectation they'd gain their freedom again.

She cleared her throat and repeated her question, positive

the mention of Keane would curb Camden's ardor as much as it did hers. "Keane disna ken about our agreement?"

Camden chuckled, his chest vibrating with his mirth.

"Nae. I have nae wish to be on the receivin' end of my cousin's wrath. I count myself fortunate he didna throttle me for marryin' ye without his blessin'." He quirked a sardonic eyebrow. "God's ballocks, can ye imagine his reaction if I told him we intended to annul the union?"

Gazing at their intertwined fingers, hers small and pale and his thick and sun-browned, she murmured, "He'd never permit me to go to Culloden with ye, and then the elopement would be exposed as a farce."

"Exactly." He squeezed her hand and winked, but his previous humor had vanished. "I always kent ye were an intelligent lass."

A long moment went by, each absorbed in their thoughts. Circumstances had irrevocably woven their together lives together in a complex tapestry: nae, a tangled knot. Even after the dissolution of their marriage, they'd no doubt encounter each other. Not only was Camden Keane's cousin and Marjorie's former brother-in-law, but he was also close to her and her daughters.

Bethea and Camden *would* see each other from time to time, unless she married another and moved away. That unwarranted thought made her positively ill.

"I must be off." With a sigh, he straightened and, at last, relinquished her hand.

An odd bereftness bathed her.

Sitting beside Camden in comfortable silence and listening to the regular rhythm of his breathing while holding his hand filled her with a deep peace and contentment.

"We'll leave as soon as I return, lass, nae matter how late

the hour." He tilted her face to his and brushed a light kiss across her lips.

Again, she felt as if he kept something from her, and she opened her mouth to ask what, but then decided against the impulse.

She stood as he did and walked with him to the door. Bethea laid a hand on his arm. "Camden. Ye will be careful, willna ye? Monteith's a deceptive snake. I dinna ken what he's capable of."

His eyes softened, the warmth in their depths doing peculiar things to her bones, and he gathered her near. She willingly stepped into his embrace. Nothing felt as natural or right as being in his arms. "I promise, Bethea."

He kissed her forehead, then her temple, then her nose, and finally settled his molded mouth upon hers. She clutched his shirt as sensation encapsulated her. One touch from this man and she forgot—well, everything.

The kiss went on and on and *on*. Hunger grew within her to know him in every way a woman could know a man. He'd only been her husband for a few hours, but already she didn't know how she'd let him go.

He drew away first, his breathing ragged. "I promise ye, lass. I'll be careful." He gave her a devilish wink. "I have a new bride and a weddin' trip to look forward to."

Then he was gone.

Bethea stood there with one hand on her heart and her fingertips touching her still throbbing lips as a shocking, wholly inconceivable thought kept repeating in her mind over and over and over.

I dinna want an annulment.

ELEVEN

Parkhill Hall
Edinburgh, Scotland
Late Afternoon
23 March 1721

The next day, his temper simmering and frustration boiling, Camden was shown into the green parlor once more. He'd noticed three trunks and a valise in the entryway, no doubt Bethea's things.

He'd stopped at his lodgings long enough to pack his few belongings, which easily fit into a small valise. He never packed much when on a mission, for he needed to be able to move at a moment's notice. His bag sat in the foyer beside Bethea's.

Camden had also penned a letter to Bryston, asking him to investigate a growing suspicion. One that infuriated and worried him. If Camden was correct about Makepeace's treachery, His Majesty King George I should be informed at once. The unsealed missive lay tucked inside his coat pocket to give to Keane.

Upon discovering that someone tipped Monteith off, and

the traitor had fled the city sometime in the early morning hours, Keane had returned to the house yesterday afternoon.

Camden only needed one guess to know who'd prospered most from the situation.

They'd been idiots to ever use the mercenaries, but Sir Walter had insisted. Which, in truth, was a departure from his tendency to reject anything and anyone who wasn't strictly appropriate. Highly suspicious and worth investigating.

Camden had spent the last four-and-twenty hours scouring every place Monteith might've scuttled to hide, to no avail. Infuriated, or so he'd acted, Sir Walter had returned to London with instructions for Camden to lay low and await word from him.

Marjorie bustled in carrying a full tray herself, rather than having a servant do so. "You must be starving, Camden. Sit down and eat. I doubt you've had a bite since yesterday."

It was true. He'd gulped down a bowl of porridge and a piece of black bread at The Boar and Brew Inn yesterday morning.

Bethea had only nibbled an oatcake and sipped tea.

He regretted having to bundle her back into a coach for a longer journey today, but if the tracks weren't overly muddy, they'd only have to stay one night at an inn. Under false identities, naturally.

It made him nervous as hell that Monteith was on the loose and likely knew Bethea had revealed everything she'd heard about him. It came as no surprise that the compartment in the earl's study was as empty as a beggar's purse.

What he wouldn't give to know what the contents had been.

"How is Bethea?" he asked, sinking into a chair and gratefully accepting the plate of food Marjorie shoved toward him.

Repeatedly, the past few hours, his mind had returned to

Bethea. It was a distraction an agent of the Crown couldn't afford, which was why so few were married. Already, he pondered if he would continue as an operative. Quelling another rising had been his primary concern, and now that goal had been achieved.

His empty stomach growled loudly, and Marjorie arched a sardonic brow. "Eat. She'll be down shortly." Her expression softened. "And she's fine, Camden. Bethea's no wilting flower. She a strong woman."

Aye, he'd seen her strength. Her intelligence and calm reasoning too.

Not many women would've endured what she had and not dissolved into tears or histrionics. Throughout her ordeal, she'd shown courage and temperance that he couldn't help but admire.

It was when a person was under the most stress their true character emerged, and what he'd discovered about Bethea impressed him all the more. She was a woman a man would be proud and privileged to call his wife.

And she *was* his wife.

A stroke of luck or fate?

He'd just set his fork aside when Bethea entered wearing a dark green traveling costume and carrying a heavy velvet cloak. "I'm ready to depart whenever ye are," she said, drawing on a black kid glove. A slight crease between her eyebrows, she roved her gaze over him. "Ye look exhausted."

Camden shrugged as he cut a piece of sirloin. "'Tis no' the first time I've gone without sleep."

From the fine lines bracketing her mouth, Camden would wager Keane had told her about Monteith's escape. She needed to know. It was her right.

There was no reason to suppose Monteith would exact revenge on her, and yet Camden couldn't dispel his unease.

From what Etherington had revealed, as well as Camden's observations, the earl's obsession with Bethea bordered on unhinged.

Keane strode into the salon at that precise moment and offered an austere upward sweep of his mouth.

"I've arranged to have four men inconspicuously follow the coach. I've also hired an unmarked conveyance but have assigned two of my best men to drive." His gaze gravitated to Bethea's pale face, and he offered an encouraging smile. "Just a precaution, lass. I doubt the earl is still in Scotland."

To her credit, she notched her chin up and straightened her spine. "As long as Camden is with me, I'm no' worried."

The trust she put in him humbled and scared the hell out of him.

Casting a glance to the window, he took in a sky gray from coal smoke and rain clouds before examining the mantel clock. He wiped his mouth, then rose. "We'd best be off."

"Wait. Please." Branwen limped into the room with the aid of her cane. "I want to say farewell." Her gait uneven, she thumped toward her sister, but Bethea rushed to meet her.

"Can ye see this posted for me?" Camden pulled the letter from his coat pocket and extended it to Keane. "Read it first. There's information included ye should be aware of."

That brought Keane's eyebrows crashing together. Nevertheless, he accepted the folded paper and firmed his mouth in assent.

Branwen glanced at Keane and then to Camden. "I wish we didna have to remain in Edinburgh."

"Ye canna travel with yer injured feet, darlin'." Bethea drew her intrigued regard from the letter and smiled at her sister. "We'll be together soon. A month will fly by. Ye'll see." She kissed Branwen's cheek and hugged her.

Both Keane and Marjorie also kissed Bethea. After

embracing her, Marjorie tucked her hand into the bend of Keane's arm and gave a subtle squeeze.

He was truly beside himself with concern. For a man who'd had the guardianship of two girls thrust upon him when he'd barely been a man himself, he'd risen to the occasion admirably. The affection between the Glanville sisters and their guardian was obvious.

They were a family.

Camden clasped Keane's hand. "I'll keep her safe, Cousin."

"I ken ye will."

Ten minutes later, Camden and Bethea left Edinburgh behind and rumbled toward a future he'd never anticipated.

Bethea was silent, and although she didn't seem fretful, he sensed she wasn't at ease either.

"Are ye all right, Bethea?"

She turned from staring out the window and curved her pretty mouth. "Aye. I'm tryin' to figure out who would've alerted Monteith. Do ye think it was one of the mercenaries?"

"I'd bet on it," he said.

Likely Anderson. What Camden didn't know for certain was if Sir Walter was somehow involved. His gut told him he was.

Bethea returned her attention to the passing scenery. Shadows were starting to elongate the trees. "How far will we travel?"

"I'd like to put as many miles between Edinburgh and us as possible."

"Mmm." She made a soft sound that was impossible to interpret.

To lighten the mood, he cocked his head. "What shall we call ourselves when we arrive at the inn?"

She faced him again, her eyes bright. "I've always liked the name Moria."

"And I'll be... *Hamish*?"

"That's too predictable." She wrinkled her adorable nose. "Isna there a name ye've always liked that's a little unusual?"

"One of my middle names is Tavin."

"Tavin." She tried it on her tongue. "I like it." Grinning, Bethea nodded. She'd lowered her hood hours ago, and the loose curls at her temple pirouetted with the motion. "So we are Moria and Tavin, *what*?"

He put a finger to his chin in mock concentration. "Somethin' common, I think. Smith? Brown? Johnson? Thomson?"

"Thomson." She pulled her gloves off and tucked them into her cloak's pocket. "Are we still newlyweds, or should we pretend to have been married longer in case someone comes lookin' for a newlywed couple?"

"Why, Mrs. Kennedy. Are ye enjoyin' this misadventure?"

"Well, ye must admit 'tis excitin'."

Not the word he'd use, but the color had returned to her cheeks, and her silver-gray eyes sparkled with anticipation. He'd not tell her about the concerns flitting around his mind.

Leaning back, Camden folded his arms. "Well, since I canna keep my eyes off ye, nae one is goin' to credit we've been married verra long."

She flushed and darted her tongue out to moisten her lower lip.

God's teeth, she's a temptress.

He swallowed a groan and adjusted his position on the seat so that she couldn't see his growing cock. This marriage of convenience was becoming more and more inconvenient with each passing mile.

"Uh, hum. I ken what ye mean." She gave him a flirtatious

glance from beneath her lashes. "Ye arena so bad to gaze upon yerself."

He needed to change the direction of the conversation, or this marriage would be consummated in short order and in a manner nae bride deserved. Tupped on a carriage seat by an overzealous husband.

"If anyone asks, we've been married for three months," he said. "That's long enough to deter suspicion."

She nodded and fell silent, though she ran her fingertips up and down the edge of her cloak, revealing she wasn't as calm inwardly as she pretended to be.

"Och, what is on yer mind, lass?"

She turned those beautiful, intelligent pewter gray eyes upon him. Why hadn't he noticed the flecks of blue and purple in them, before?

"I'm just wonderin' how long we'll have to pretend to be married." She gave him a rueful smile. "I ken ye have responsibilities to the Crown. Where will I live while ye are—"

Before she could object, he crossed the coach and after sitting beside her, pulled her onto his lap. She issued a startled squeak, but settled against his chest.

"We'll cross those bridges when we come to them, Bethea."

Not that he hadn't already been thinking of ideas and then tossing them aside almost as quickly as he'd contrived them. The only future he imagined now was one with Bethea.

In fact, he meant to do whatever he must to convince her to remain his wife.

Her lashes lowered partway, but not before he saw her glance at his mouth.

Male satisfaction tunneled through him.

"Bethea?"

"Aye?" She tilted her neck to look at him.

Aye, definitely purple flecks in her now smokey gray eyes, and those amethyst shards glittered when she was aroused. Camden tucked that fascinating fact into the back of his mind.

"I'm goin' to kiss ye unless ye tell me no' to."

Her chin angled up a bit more, and she leaned into him.

"Why, Camden, would I do that?"

Then he yielded to the fire smoldering in his blood and took her sweet mouth, tasting her essence, and wishing she might be his for all time.

TWELVE

Dirk and Duck Inn
Midway between Edinburgh and Culloden
23 March 1721

Long after the sun had set and only the purplish-dark blue of impending night streaked the northern sky, the coach jostled and groaned to a stop in the circular dirt courtyard before a two-story structure. The ground floor's curtained windows glowed with muted light.

A half-moon hung lazily in the sky, visible now and again as fat, lazy clouds drifted past. A large brown and white dog, its tail wagging, barked an exuberant greeting as it jumped to its feet on the stoop.

Squinting, Bethea tried to read the sign swaying softly in the breeze.

Dirk and Duck?

That was supposed to be a duck? It looked more like a sickly stork, or mayhap an oversized crow a child had painted.

A sagging front step and lopsided shutters suggested the establishment wasn't as well kept as The Boar and Brew. She eyed the lodging house warily as Camden handed her down before he reached in and collected her valise with her overnight necessities.

"Have ye stayed here before?" she asked, trying to keep the apprehension from her tone.

"Nae. I thought it wiser to stay at an inn where nae one would know me." Camden glanced around, then nodded in silent communication to a coachman.

That made sense. They were traveling incognito, after all, and this lodging house was certainly off the beaten path.

Would the coachmen and the other riders Keane had sent to safeguard them sleep inside the inn too? She rather hoped they would. She supposed it depended on how many chambers were available though.

From the rundown looks of the place, it didn't host an abundance of travelers regularly.

Two tow-headed stable lads, one carrying a lamp, both sporting broad grins on their well-scrubbed faces, trotted out to greet the drivers and team.

"I'd like ye to sleep near the coach tonight," Camden advised the two armed coachmen.

Ah, so he, too, had noticed the seedier elements of the hostelry. Bethea prayed that at least the linens were clean.

"Aye," Higgins, the burlier of the drivers, agreed, giving the inn a once-over. "'Tis a good idea."

Crawley, the other coachman, spoke quietly with one of the lads as they prepared to unhitch the team.

"Pull yer hood up, lass," Camden advised even as he rucked his coat collar higher and pulled his hat lower. "We dinna ken who might be inside."

She complied without complaint.

"Camden, are ye certain...?" Before Bethea finished the sentence, the four unofficial guards rode into the courtyard, two abreast. *It will be fine,* she consoled herself. Counting these four, the drivers who looked like they could take on a bear single-handedly, and Camden, they were well protected.

It wasn't in her nature to be high-strung, nervous, or suspicious, but then again, she'd never been a witness to treason or abducted before. Not to mention wedding under duress and then fleeing under an assumed name to evade possible retaliation by said traitor.

Another stable boy, this one younger and with darker hair, hastily tucked his slightly too-big shirt into his breeches as he hurried from the stables and went directly to the newcomers. "Welcome to the Dirk and Duck," he greeted cheerily.

Well, at least the stable hands were an efficient and merry lot in their clean, but obviously worn and mended, clothing.

In short order, Camden had ushered Bethea inside and secured a chamber for them. She didn't protest when he requested one room rather than two.

She didn't fear he'd force himself upon her, and in truth, she'd not sleep a wink if alone in a chamber in this strange place, knowing Monteith was out *there* somewhere.

A couple of nondescript men—the only occupants of the public room—nursed tankards of ale. They conversed in low tones at a slightly uneven table a few feet from the fireplace.

Their footsteps heavy on the wood floor, the guards entered and, conversing in low tones, awaited their turn to speak with the innkeeper.

"Did my lads see to yer horses?" the innkeeper asked.

"Aye, and most efficiently too," Camden replied with an easy smile. "There'll be a generous tip for them come morn."

The thin man smiled, pride evident in his wide grin. "'Tis just me, the three lads, and my two daughters. The missus died a couple of years ago, but the lasses ken how to cook a decent meal and keep the place clean. My youngest lad painted the inn's sign."

Parental pride expanded his chest.

A child *had* painted the sign.

A stab of remorse pricked Bethea for judging so quickly. The poor man was trying to support his family the best way he knew how, and she'd found fault before she knew anything of their circumstances.

Another surreptitious look revealed he spoke the truth.

The lodging-house was quite humble, but the floor was swept clean and looked well-scrubbed, the tables were wiped, and no cobwebs collected dust in the corners. A hearty fire burned in the oversized fireplace dominating the public room.

A bright-eyed lass of about sixteen years emerged from what must've been the kitchen and placed steaming bowls of stew, several thick slices of bread, butter, and cheese before the men. They tucked into the simple fair with gusto.

With a polite nod, she brushed her hands together and made straight for her father.

"This is Kate," the innkeeper announced. "She'll see yer stomachs are full."

The proprietor turned his attention to the four men patiently waiting behind Camden and Bethea, acting for all the world as if they were strangers rather than armed guards sent to protect them.

"My coachmen need food and ale," Camden said to Kate. "They intend to stay with the coach and team tonight."

"I'll see to it." She nodded, her freckled face breaking into a friendly smile. "What about ye and yer lady?"

"My wife is travel-weary," Camden said without a flicker of unease at the fib. He took Bethea's elbow. "We'll eat in our chamber."

"Verra good, sir. Either Mattie or I will bring yer food to ye and water for washin'."

The other sister, Bethea presumed.

Kate bobbed a shallow curtsy and hurried to the kitchen.

"Our room is on this level," Camden whispered in her ear as he guided her to an adjacent corridor. "I prefer ground floors when stayin' someplace I'm no' familiar. 'Tis easier to escape."

Once a spy, always a spy.

Bethea had scarcely removed her cloak before a light knock at the door announced the arrival of supper.

Camden answered and directed Mattie to place the tray on a table situated below a window. Kate followed her sister and poured warm water into the basin.

"Let us ken if ye need anythin' else," Kate offered with another genial smile.

They were certainly happy children, despite the loss of their mother.

And they were so eager to please that it pulled at Bethea's heartstrings. She made a mental note to advise Keane to send travelers this way. Perhaps Camden would do the same, as well as his brother, Graeme.

"My cloak could use brushin' and my shoes cleaned," Bethea offered on impulse. "If ye have time. I'd pay ye, of course."

The lasses bobbed their heads.

"Of course, we can," Mattie assured.

Smiling broadly, they left the chamber a few minutes later, carrying not only her cloak and shoes but Camden's boots as well.

Another piece of her heart fell at his feet.

At this rate, he'd possess the whole organ before they reached Culloden.

Considering him, she finished drying her hands. He was certainly easy on the eyes. Head tilted, she pointed a finger at him after he shut the door. "Why, Camden Kennedy, yer as soft-hearted as I am."

He chuckled and rolled a shoulder. "I'll leave a generous tip. I admire a man who works hard and has taught his children to do so as well."

"I thought I'd ask Keane to send a bit of business their way," she said, fingering the embroidery along the edge of the linen provided for drying.

Approval in his eyes, he bent his strong mouth into a disarming grin. "I had a similar thought."

Plink. And there went another piece of her heart.

You, Bethea Reganne Margaret Glanville, are in big trouble.

"That smells marvelous." Sniffing appreciatively, Camden strode to the basin to wash his hands, passing much too close to Bethea for her already heightened senses. Every nerve was strung taut as a violin string, and awareness hummed between them.

Suddenly the room felt entirely too small, and the bed entirely too big.

"Venison stew, I believe." Bethea concentrated on setting out the food before arranging the serviettes and utensils. Anything to keep her wanton mind off him. She slipped onto a chair and unfolded her napkin.

He joined her at the table, and she couldn't help but reflect on what a domesticated scene they presented.

As Bethea swallowed her first bite of surprisingly flavorful stew, she realized just how hungry she was. She'd had little appetite after the hasty ceremony. Had it only been this morning that she and Camden had reluctantly exchanged vows?

Bethea had come to know so much about him in such a short time. It seemed as if she'd known him for years. In truth, she was as comfortable in his presence as Keane's, except for the electric sexual undercurrent that ebbed and flowed between them.

It was always there, lingering just beneath the surface and easily sparked to life at the slightest innocent touch, smoldering glance, or seductive timbre of his voice.

Her spoon resting in her bowl, Bethea paused and studied Camden. Neck bent, he applied himself to the meal with great exuberance. At Trentwick Castle, she'd seen just how much he'd eaten to satisfy a man of his size and build. Likely, he was half-starved, given the minimal amount he'd consumed today.

Lord, but he was a spectacular specimen of manhood. Since first meeting him, she'd thought Camden handsome, but something in her perspective of him had shifted. She viewed him through new lenses now, and she very much liked what she saw.

He was *her* husband.

True, the arrangement was temporary, but somehow the knowledge that they were husband and wife seemed to have awoken a feminine part of her—a womanly part, very much conscious of him as a virile man. And now she couldn't stop thinking about his scorching kisses or wondering what it would be like to be his wife in every way.

Her nipples hardened as heat pooled low in her belly.

Cease.

Such musings were unwise.

She and Camden couldn't consummate the marriage, or else there'd be no annulment. Aye, they might share a mutual, carnal attraction, but neither was prepared for *until death do us part.*

Was *she?*

He glanced up from his food, his fork in midair. "What?"

Caught staring like a goose.

"Nothin'." Revealing heat stole up her cheeks even as she shook her head. She cursed that she easily blushed. The dratted affliction made it nearly impossible to conceal her feelings.

His well-formed mouth spread into a charmer's smile.

Bethea had always disdained calf-eyed females who wore their hearts on their sleeves, and here she was acting the silliest of ninnies.

His gaze darkened seductively as he looked over the brim of his wine glass and took a long swallow.

She forbid her focus to gravitate to his corded neck. Was there any part of Camden Kennedy that wasn't enticing sculpted muscle and tempting sinewy contours? How was any woman not in her dotage supposed to remain immune to that male perfection?

"Bethea?"

His timbre held arousal, and something significantly more tantalizing.

Lord, she was in trouble.

Refusing to look up or else her eyes might give her innermost thoughts away, she slathered butter on a piece of bread and affected indifference. She didn't even like butter. "Hmm?"

"Bethea?"

Just the way her name rolled off his tongue sent tingles to unmentionable places.

The wine glass made a light clink as he set it down. "Look at me."

She shook her head, her attention riveted on her food. "I dinna think that's a verra good idea."

"Why?" His voice sounded like warm, smooth honey. Rich and delicious and tempting. So, so tempting.

Good God.

Could that damned brogue sound any sexier? His words entwined around her, sensuous and intoxicating. Bethea was on the verge of throwing herself into his arms and demanding he have his way with her. Or that *she* have her way with *him.*

She was *not* answering that question.

What would she say?

Camden, just yer voice has me quivering with carnal need.

A very strong suspicion nagged that he knew precisely how he affected her.

His chair scraped unnaturally loudly as he scooted it back, but she kept her attention trained on her food. One touch, one word, and the self-restraint she barely held in check would shatter. Scatter like thistledown in a windstorm.

When had she become so malleable?

How could she want Camden this much? For surely, that was what this feeling—this aching, burning need. Bethea didn't even know what exactly she wanted but instinctively knew he could provide it.

Ye didna wish to marry him, she sternly reminded herself.

Her lustful self tittered, *Aye, but ye want to bed him.*

This is only temporary.

Dinna let yer emotions become involved.

She closed her eyes in an attempt to ignore the hulking man towering over her and her immediate, intense response.

Too late. Too late. Too dashed late.

Still holding the bread, she seized her wine goblet and took a deep drink, wishing it was something stronger to steady her nerves.

As he gently removed the bread from her shaking fingertips, she swallowed. Just as tenderly, he drew her to her feet, one hand cradling her waist and the other cupping her nape.

"Ye ken, I want ye, and I ken ye want me too, *leannan.*"

Sweetheart.

With each husky word, he dipped his midnight dark head lower and lower.

Lord help her, she was utterly and completely lost.

His mouth took possession of Bethea's, hot and urgent and hungry.

This was inevitable. She'd known it since Camden had stood in the chamber at The Boar and Brew. And had fought it every minute since saying "I do."

With a moan of surrender, she sank into Camden's embrace and, standing on her toes, wrapped her arms around the wall of his back and returned his kisses.

She opened her mouth and met his tongue with her own. Thrusting and parrying, a duel of passion and need.

He tasted of wine and Camden.

A primal, possessive growl throttling up his throat, he scooped her into his arms and, with their mouths still clinging together, carried her to the bed. He lay her down, and a second later, the mattress dipped as he stretched out beside her.

She swallowed at his bronzed, masculine beauty.

Bunching her skirts up, he brushed one big hand up her thigh to her hip. "Yer so bonnie, lass," Camden murmured throatily between smoldering kisses along her jaw, throat, and behind her neck.

Who knew that spot could turn her bones to warm custard?

Every part of her wanted this, wanted to submit to the bliss she instinctively knew he would give her. And every part of her also shrieked a warning.

If Bethea joined with him, she'd give him more than her body. Her heart would be his as well. She'd always known that truth for herself. And at this moment, her fear of the future and the unknown outweighed the lust coursing through her.

Her heart and mind racing, passion warring with logic, she lay perfectly still.

She couldn't do this.

Couldn't submit to the sensual assault.

As much as her body wanted her to, and much as she wanted to experience Camden's touch and give herself to him, take him into her, she simply couldn't.

"Camden?" She touched his jaw, trying to ignore the delicious flutters in her belly and the swelling of her aching breasts.

"Aye, lass?" He brushed a thumb across her nipple as if he knew she needed that touch.

She nearly cried out with her pleasure.

Again. Do it again.

And he did, but this time, he rolled her nipple between his fingers.

God almighty. The air escaped her lungs on a harsh woosh, and she pressed her palms to his chest and shoved. If she didn't stop now, she was lost. "I'm sorry, but we canna do this."

He went still at once, his hard maleness pulsing against her thigh. He blew out a breath and levered himself upright. "Aye. Yer right. Forgive me. I never intended it to go this far." He gave a self-depreciatory chuckle as he fingered a curl. "Once I kissed ye..."

"An inferno ignited," she murmured, voicing her thoughts about her reaction.

"For ye too?"

She nodded and whispered, "Aye, but if we make love, we'd be married in truth."

"Would that be so bad?" His intense blue eyes searched hers, probing, seeking.

She swallowed and averted her gaze. "I dinna ken, but I canna let a moment of lust dictate my future."

He rose, and she felt him gazing down at her.

Did he think her a tease? A wanton?

Why did she want to curl into a ball and cry?

Because she'd almost given herself to him?

Or because she didn't dare?

"I'm goin' to check on the drivers," he said softly, his burr thick with regret and remorse. "I'll sleep in the corridor. Try to sleep, Bethea."

Not likely. Not when confusion swirled inside her like a dervish. And not when common sense had denied her what her heart and soul desperately wanted.

A moment later, the door clicked shut.

Turning onto her side, Bethea buried her face in the pillow and burst into tears.

THIRTEEN

Glen Toramallan Lodge
Outside Culloden
Eighteen days later-10 April 1721

Whistling under his breath, Camden tramped up the path from Brooke Toram. In one hand, he carried a fishing pole, and in the other, five large, brown trout—tonight's dinner.

The sometimes-fickle Highland spring had chosen benevolence today, and the sun shone gloriously in a crystal blue, cloudless sky. Two shy does eyed him curiously from beneath a lonely Scots pine, and an early graceful yellow and black butterfly flitted among the grasses.

As he neared Glen Toramallan Lodge, a husky contralto singing *Adieu, Dundee* carried to him from behind the house, and he grinned.

Like yon water softly gliding,
When the winds are laid to sleep
Such my life, when I confiding
Gave to her my heart to keep.
Bethea.

She liked to sing as she kneaded bread, picked flowers, or strolled the overgrown garden paths. That she couldn't carry a tune in a handbasket made no difference to her. She unashamedly hummed or sang one ballad after another, just for the joy it brought her.

Crawley and Higgins nodded a greeting as they brushed the matching blacks. For all of their casual demeanor, they took in everything happening around them.

Two of the other men, Stevens and Leech, had assumed roles as footmen. Hulking, awkward, and unsophisticated footmen, in truth. The remaining two guards, Hetrick and Livingston, tended the grounds and patrolled the hundred-acre estate. All six took turns guarding the main house in pairs at night as well.

In addition to hiring a cook, Mrs. Mary Newberry, who came in the morning and left after dinner, two village lasses, Alice and Brigette, had taken positions as maids. Glen Toramallen consisted of almost thirty rooms, and despite the female employees, Bethea frequently helped with the baking and cleaning.

Since arriving at Glen Toramallan, nothing suspicious had occurred, and Camden hoped they hadn't all been lulled into a false sense of security. He watched for a letter daily from Keane, Bryston, or even Sir Walter, updating him. Thus far, no missive had arrived, which wasn't unusual, given the irregularity of the post.

And yet, an undercurrent of unease wouldn't let him relax and kept him alert.

In all likelihood, Monteith now called a cell his home, if he hadn't lost his head as yet. The same could be said of Etherington. The one piece of the puzzle that continued to nag like a drunken fishwife was Sir Walter Makepeace.

He swore the man was keeping something from him.

But what? Hopefully, Bryston would find out.

Bethea's voice rang out louder as he rounded the corner of the house.

Like yon water wildly rushing
When the north wind stirs the sea,
Such the change my heart now crushing,
Love, adieu! adieu, Dundee.

A basket of wildflowers in one hand, she twirled in a circle before dropping a curtsy to a trio of black-faced sheep watching her in fascination in the adjacent meadow. Today she wore a blue and yellow gown, as cheerful as the Highland spring day. As she often did, she'd fashioned her hair into a simple chignon with a ribbon wound around her crown and tied at the nape.

He drank her in, from the slopes of her cheeks to the graceful arch of her back. A woodland nymph. That was what she was, and she'd thoroughly enchanted him. Stolen what he hadn't already given her of his heart.

"So, ye've taken to singin' to beasties, have ye?"

Camden strolled forward, unable to check his delighted grin. With each passing day, Bethea had wiggled her way further and further into his heart, until she'd set up house there. And he couldn't begin to imagine his life without her. If she left, nothing and no one could or would fill the empty space she'd leave.

He'd redoubled his efforts to woo her, and in the past few days, from the soft smiles and frequent glances she sent his way, his gentle offensive appeared to be working.

"Aye, indeed." Instead of blushing in chagrin, she flashed him a mischievous smile and bobbed another curtsy. "They dinna seem to care that I dinna have a voice." She angled her head and spoke to the sheep. "Do ye?"

One bobbed its head, and Bethea burst out laughing. "I

dinna ken whether to be insulted or amused." She caught sight of the trout. "I see yer fishin' expedition was successful."

"Aye." He'd used it as an excuse to walk the estate and check for himself that no one suspicious loitered nearby. In just over a week, they were to return home. Although, he still hadn't initiated a discussion with Bethea about where, exactly, they would live.

In truth, he wouldn't mind remaining here, but Glen Toramallan belonged to Keane. Perhaps it was the peace and happiness Camden wanted to last, this false sense of normalcy. He and Bethea had settled into a comfortable routine, very much like a typical married couple.

The single exception was he'd forbidden himself to make any advances toward her sexually. If their marriage were ever consummated, it would be because she initiated it.

Camden wouldn't have her live with regrets for the rest of her life.

He touched her often, holding her hand on occasion, and dropping a kiss on her forehead every night before she sought her bed. At which time, he sought Brooke Toram's frigid waters to cool his ardor. He'd never had his restraint so sorely tested before.

He well understood her reluctance, and yet he had no doubt she wanted him. He'd seen her looking at him, recognized the signs of a woman whose passions had been stirred. And yet she held herself back.

She needed more time.

That was the quandary, however. The more Camden contemplated it, the more he'd come to accept that if their marriage were annulled, it needed to be sooner rather than later. A scandal couldn't be avoided, and the longer they waited to petition for a dissolution of the marriage, the less likely it would be granted.

Divorce remained an option, but those weren't easily obtained either.

If nothing else, these past days had confirmed his belief that Bethea was the woman for him, and he wanted her to remain his wife. Time was running out to convince her of that, however.

"Why the long face?" she asked, coming to stand beside him and peering upward.

"Nothin'." He shook his head. "I was just wonderin' why we havena had any word from Keane or Bryston. I expected a letter by now."

"Aye." A shadow flitted across her face, and her eyelashes fluttered downward. "I'm sure yer anxious to put this behind ye, and accept yer next mission."

He bent his head near, drawing a startled glance from her. "Nae, I dinna think a married man ought to take such risks. I've decided to resign my position."

"Have ye now?" She bit her full lower lip and adjusted the basket.

Camden couldn't quite determine what caused the slight catch in her voice and sparkle in her eye. *Hope?*

He stepped closer until his thighs touched hers through her gown, giving her time to retreat or rebuff him. Instead, she wet her lower lip, and her gray eyes softened in invitation.

That was all the encouragement he needed.

Grateful the kitchens were located on the house's other side, and they weren't visible from the stables, he greedily took her mouth.

Bethea sank into him, opening her lips and accepting his tongue with an eagerness that stoked his desire higher and higher.

She tasted of raspberries and tea, and her floral scent entwined around him, inflaming his passion into an uncontrollable firestorm. Kissing her wasn't enough, but with his hands full, he couldn't encircle her in his arms and press her against the house's rock side. Couldn't ruck her skirts up and explore the satiny flesh and rounded curves he'd dreamed of every night.

With a frustrated groan, he raised his head and waved his arms up and down. "I picked a terrible time to kiss ye."

Her eyes rather dreamy, and her plump lips pink from his kisses, she curved her mouth. "Nae time ye kiss me is terrible, Camden."

Something in her tone gave him pause, and he shifted the pole to his other hand, awkwardly gripping the fish and pole in one fist. He pulled her to him and savored her mouth again. "I'd do much more than kiss ye every day for the rest of my life if ye'd let me," he murmured into her hair.

"Wouldna ye have regrets?" Head angled, her perceptive gaze probed his. "I couldna bear that."

Cupping her nape with his free hand, he shook his head before pressing his forehead to hers. "Nae. No' a one. Marryin' ye was the smartest thing I've ever done, *mo ghaol.*"

My love.

She *was* his love.

The keeper of his marauder's heart. The other half of his whole. He couldn't regret their forced marriage or a single moment he'd spent with her since.

"Ahem."

A very exaggerated throat clearing jerked Camden back to reality. He glanced toward the corner of the house. Higgins, red-faced but wearing a sloppy grin, stood there, letters in his hand. "These only just arrived, and I kent ye were awaitin' word."

Camden gave Bethea's shoulder a slight, apologetic

squeeze. He'd have explored what this was blossoming between them much further.

She seemed as reluctant as he to separate.

He curved an arm about her waist and gently urged her toward Higgins.

Her cheeks glowed pink, but she gave Higgins a bright smile.

As soon as he'd handed Camden the letter, he touched his forehead and beat a hasty retreat. Every one of the other men would know of Camden's infatuation with his wife within ten minutes.

And he didn't give twenty tinkers' damns.

"Who are they from?" Bethea fell into step beside him, leaning into his side as if it were the most natural thing to do.

Such love swirled inside Camden at the simple, trusting gesture that his throat tightened. His heart lay at her feet, to be trampled, or picked up and treasured. He sure as hell didn't know what he'd ever done to deserve this remarkable woman, but he thanked God she was his.

Somehow, he must convince her to remain so.

He thumbed through them. "Bryston, Keane, and..." He turned the third letter over and missed a step before coming to an abrupt halt upon recognizing the extravagant seal. "*The king.*"

FOURTEEN

Bethea stared at the letters in Camden's sun-browned hand as they approached the kitchen entrance. Just short of the door, she placed her palm atop his.

"Camden, please dinna open them yet."

He met her gaze, a question in his arresting blue eyes.

Her heart racing madly at her boldness for what she was about to do, she managed a tremulous smile. "They might change everythin', and..." She felt the color heating her cheeks, but she bravely raised her chin. If she didn't do this now, she mightn't ever. "And before they do, I would be yer wife in every way. If ye'll have me, and if that's what ye desire too."

Without argument, he tucked the letters into his jacket pocket.

"Aye, I'll gladly have ye, Bethea Kennedy." His eyes filled with primal satisfaction as a seductive grin crooked his mouth. "Today and every day, for the rest of my life." He glanced down at the fish and rod and chuckled. "Let me dispose of these, and then we can have a *proper* conversation."

Her tummy toppled over in giddy expectation. She sincerely doubted they'd be conversing in words, and a delicious thrill started in her middle and spread outward. For days she'd attempted to muster the courage to tell Camden she wanted him in her bed. Wanted to remain his wife. Yet each time she'd opened her mouth to tell him, her courage had fled.

It wasn't the *forever, till death do us part* piece that kept her tongue-tied.

It was the fear he hadn't come to care for her, to love her as she had him these past weeks. For she'd admitted to herself several days ago what she'd suspected since the day she'd married him—Camden Kennedy had captured her heart. And with each grin, each kiss to her forehead, each charming or rakish comment or chuckle, the organ became more firmly cemented at his feet.

She'd found herself humming and singing, which in truth, was cruelty to humanity and animal-kind since she well knew she held no talent in that direction. Nevertheless, her joy demanded a venue of expression, and she could hardly dance about the house or lawns. Although... she'd been doing just that when he'd come upon her a few minutes ago.

She swung the basket of flowers, drawing his attention to the early blooms she'd cut from the now tidy gardens beds, thanks to Hetrick and Livingston. "I'll just leave these in the kitchen."

After bracing his fishing pole next to the house, Camden kissed her temple before opening the door. At once, warmth and the aromas of dried herbs, fresh bread, and whatever was cooking engulfed her.

Glen Toramallan's kitchen, as well as the rest of the house, sparkled after a thorough cleaning by Mrs. Newberry, the maids, and Bethea. Though the lodge didn't quite feel like home, the house was comfortable and welcoming.

Mrs. Newberry looked up from stirring a pot atop the stove, a smile wreathing her plump face. A lock of red hair peeking out from beneath her cap clung to her damp forehead.

"Och, look at those fat fish," she exclaimed in admiration with an approving nod. "'Tis baked trout for dinner tonight." Angling her head, she indicated a large bowl atop a table. "Ye can leave them there, sir."

As Camden deposited the fish, Bethea set the basket on another table.

"Either Bridget or Alice can place these in vases in the dinin' and mornin' rooms," she suggested.

"Aye, Mrs. Kennedy."

How Bethea loved hearing that. What had started as a desperate lie had become a most treasured reality.

Mrs. Newberry sprinkled an herb into the fragrant, bubbling pot, then lifted the spoon a few inches. "Leek and potato soup to accompany the fish."

"Wonderful." Camden placed his hand at the small of Bethea's back and swiftly ushered her from the kitchen. "Trout and soup are no' what I'm hungry for," he fairly purred into her ear.

Lord. Just hearing his voice pouring over her like warm honey unhinged Bethea's knees.

"Och, young love." Mrs. Newberry's chuckle lengthened into the paneled corridor.

Good heavens, did *she* know what Bethea and Camden were going to do?

Clasping her hand in his, as eager as a schoolboy about to embark on a grand adventure, he pulled her to the stairs. She giggled when, at the top of the landing, he swung her into his arms.

"Camden," she admonished, her voice bubbling with mirth and adoration. "Someone will see."

"Aye," he concurred with a sinful grin and equally wicked wink. "And likely hear too, if I am as skilled as I think I am."

She went hot to her toes and wondered precisely what he meant, though she had a fair notion. Rather than succumbing to embarrassment, Bethea quite looked forward to whatever would cause such a reaction.

"Yer chamber or mine, Wife?"

"Och, I..."

"Mine," he decided succinctly, striding swiftly along the corridor. "'Tis farther from the kitchen and servant's quarters, for I mean to make ye cry my name as ye come undone."

That sounded very spectacular, indeed.

Looping her arms about his neck, Bethea giggled again. "'Tis no' even twelve of the clock yet. What will the servants say?"

"'About bloody time,'" he growled, lowering his head to nuzzle her throat. "And I have to agree. I've wanted this since I kissed ye at The Boar and Brew. Nae, before. When I danced with ye at the Hogmanay celebration."

She grinned and kissed his corded neck, earning another rough sound from him. "Mmm."

He smelled divine: spices, and musky male, and the outdoors.

"Stop that, or I'll no' make it to my chamber, and I'd no' take ye against the wall our first time."

She arched her neck, searching his eyes. "Is that possible?"

"Aye, 'tis."

"Och, my." Bethea tried to envision exactly what that might entail. The image was quite erotic. "I think I should like to try it."

"No' this time," he denied firmly. "This time, I'll have ye naked and in my bed, in my arms so I can worship ye in the manner ye deserve. I'll take my time introducin' ye to passion, *mo ghoal.*"

Her nipples pebbled and damp heat pooled between her legs. "Perhaps no' so verra much time, Camden. I fear ye may have married a wanton."

"Praise God and all the saints," came a smoldering, delighted rumble from deep within his broad chest.

Somehow, while balancing her weight in his strong arms, he managed to open his chamber door and promptly kicked it shut behind them once inside. He strode straight to the huge bed centered on one wall across from an unlit fireplace. Sunlight streamed in the wide windows, bright rays of warmth and golden light.

Bethea didn't pretend maidenly bashfulness or chagrin. She wanted this joining. Wanted to be naked and see Camden stripped bare too. Yes, virginal uncertainty niggled, but she'd not focus on that. He would show her what to do, and she welcomed the forthcoming instructions.

She presented her back. "Unlace me, please."

"With pleasure." With an adeptness she didn't wish to ponder, Camden soon had her gown sagging low on her shoulders. He brushed a hot kiss on her neck, then flicked his tongue out to taste her.

"Delicious," he murmured.

A gasp escaped her, but she only angled her head, seeking more.

With a throaty laugh that promised all sorts of wonderful things, he set her from him and stripped her gown down her arms, past her hips, and let it pool at her feet.

Between hot, wet kisses and fumbling fingertips, they stripped the clothes from each other until they stood gloriously nude before one another.

"My God," he breathed, his ravenous gaze devouring her.

Aye, indeed.

Her core tightening, she licked her lower lip.

Camden was a magnificent male animal—all sleek muscles and sinewy contours. A thick mat of pitch-black hair covered his chest before narrowing into a vee. His manhood, proud, rigid, and pulsing every little bit, jutted from a thatch of matching black hair at his groin.

Bethea's heart flipped over in her chest. This man was her husband, and hers to touch any time she wanted. To bed anytime she wanted.

Her feet carried her forward, and she caressed his face with her fingertip, then pressed her mouth to his chest. "Make me yers, Camden."

He needed no further encouragement. In a trice, they were upon the bed, and he was playing her body like a fine-tuned instrument. She gasped and panted, urging him on, growing tauter and tauter until she felt she'd shatter.

"Och, aye," she cried when he captured a nipple in his mouth while sliding his fingers amongst the damp folds of her sex.

"Ye're perfect, *mo stór*," he rasped against her aching breast. "Utterly Exquisite."

He was her darling too. For now and forever. Until the craggy Highland landscape melted into the ocean and purple heather stopped blooming.

His shaft pulsed against Bethea's thigh as she clutched him to her.

"Camden, I dinna want to wait. Please." She slid her hands down and flattened them against his tight buttocks in a silent plea. "I need ye now."

He nudged her thighs open with a knee, his hair swinging forward. Passion hardened the angle of his face, yet tenderness glinted in his eyes as he settled between her length, his turgid staff at her entrance.

"I love ye, Bethea."

Tears sprang to her eyes.

"And I love ye, Camden. So verra much."

He entered her, slowly and steadily, his immense length stretching her most erotically and deliciously. "It feels so good," she moaned into his mouth.

She tensed as a sharp, stinging pain announced he'd breached her maidenhead, but with gentle strokes of his fingers and tender kisses, he soothed her. "I promise it will only be pleasure from now on."

Instinctively, she angled her hips, and then he carried them away, soaring higher and higher with each powerful stroke, until her world collided with the sun and stars in a brilliant burst of exquisite pleasure.

As she floated back to reality, he gave one hard, final thrust, going rigid as he called her name and spilled his hot seed into her womb.

Several blissful moments passed wrapped in each other's arms as her heart and breathing returned to their normal cadence.

He rolled off her, taking her with him until she rested partially atop his torso. "Ye are mine for all time now, Bethea."

FIFTEEN

Bethea awoke sometime later and stretched like a contented cat until she realized Camden was no longer in bed. She knitted her brow, patting the cool sheets beside her to make sure.

Aye, he was gone.

Disappointment flooded Bethea as she towed the bedding up beneath her arms and lay her forearms over the folded edge. Nonetheless, a smile teased the corner of her mouth. Camden made love to her again, this time with her on top before they'd both drifted to sleep.

Camden whispered all of the tantalizing, naughty ways he wanted to take her, and even as satiated as she was, her body tingled in renewed anticipation.

The entire household likely knew they'd spent the afternoon in bed, and for the life of her, she couldn't bring herself to feel a jot of mortification. She yawned and grasped the bedding to toss it back and go in search of her husband when the chamber door swung open.

Dressed only in a kilt, shirt, and stockings, and wearing a

grin that would strip the clothing from a woman in a thrice, Camden carried a tray.

Not a doubt remained that every servant, as well as the guards, knew what they'd been about.

"I thought ye might be hungry after our bed sport," he said, shutting the door with the heel of one foot.

"Aye." Ravenous, in truth.

Bethea first fluffed the pillows and then sank into them, running her appreciative gaze over her husband. It was amazing what treasures clothing hid. Such a shame too, for she could quite easily gaze upon and explore Camden's naked form for hours—days—and never grow bored.

He set the tray on a table and then, as if it weighed no more than a downy thistle, lifted the piece and brought it to her side of the bed. A sensual smile curving his mouth, he brushed several locks of hair off her shoulder and leaned in to kiss her. "How are ye feelin'?"

She reflected for a moment. "Only a wee bit sore, but that's to be expected the first time."

"Aye." He handed her a piece of cheese and a slice of apple. "It will nae hurt again. I worried that perhaps I was a wee bit too large for ye."

"Och, that wasna a problem." Good God, was that sultry siren's voice hers? It was then that she noticed the three letters on the tray as well. Before she said anything more to puff up his already inflated manly pride, she raised an eyebrow and pointedly looked at the correspondences. "Have ye read them, then?"

Cutting a glance at the tray, he surprised her by shaking his head. He'd not tied his hair back into a queue, and he appeared every bit the marauder he'd been accused of being.

"Nae. Whatever those letters say affects ye too. We should

read them together. I want to do everthin' with ye, lass. Make all of our decisions and choices as equals and partners."

If Bethea hadn't already been head over heels in love with him, that declaration would have catapulted her into loving him. But as she already adored him, his vow just sealed her love.

She cupped his jaw, reveling in the slightly rough texture. "Ye are so verra different than any man I've ever kent." As much as she loved Keane, she couldn't conceive of him waiting to read a correspondence addressed to him until Marjorie awoke from a passion-induced nap.

Patting the mattress, she scooted over, making room for him. "Come, sit beside me. I miss touchin' ye." She glimpsed a length of muscular thigh visible below his bunched kilt. "I find I quite like gazin' at ye too." Feeling incredibly bold, she grazed a fingertip up the length of his hairy thigh, edging ever nearer to his engorged shaft.

His kilt pulsed upward, and she jerked her attention to meet his sizzling gaze. "Careful, lass, or we'll have to delay readin' the missives a wee bit longer."

Bethea bit her lip, trying to decide which she was more eager for, and at last, settled on the letters first and another rousing romp in bed afterward. "I saw a picture once in a book at Trentwick Castle, that Keane hasna idea he owns, of a man takin' a woman from behind."

His blue eyes dark as the sky before dawn, he cocked a raven eyebrow, the planes of his face becoming more defined with his arousal. He touched his beautiful mouth to hers, and she seriously reconsidered her previous words.

Perhaps making love should occur first, else how could she possibly concentrate on the letters?

"Was she kneelin' on all fours or bent over a bed? Or on

her side, with him behind her?" he asked throatily, evidently as aroused as she.

Her mouth went dry at the erotic images his words conjured, and she swallowed in an attempt to cobble together a coherent sentence. "Um, on her side, I believe."

How quickly he'd turned the tables on her, the rake.

"Ah, we'll try that first, then," he purred, as he grabbed an apple slice and the letters before wedging his large form onto the bed.

Bethea strongly suspected she'd spend much of the next few weeks naked and exploring all sorts of sexual fantasies with her husband.

What a fantastical thought.

Crunching down on the crisp fruit, he lay the letters in her lap. "Ye open them."

"But they're addressed to ye." It felt intrusive, even with his permission. She'd been taught to respect people's privacy, and correspondences most certainly were private matters.

"I'll have nae secrets between us, Bethea." He pointed a big finger at the less than crisp rectangles. "Whatever they say, we'll face together."

How had she been blessed with such a wonderful man? Biting her lower lip, she spread them out atop her thighs. "Which one first?"

Head canted, Camden considered them for a second. "Keane's."

Bethea broke the seal with a nail. "Should I read it aloud?"

"Nae. I'll read it when ye're finished." He shook his head and popped the rest of the apple into his mouth.

Bethea quickly scanned the page, then handed it to him.

He did the same. "Well, that's no' bad news. Branwen's feet have healed. Society thinks our elopement verra romantic and nae gossipmongers are banterin' our names about."

"And they'll return to Trentwick by the end of the month." She refolded the letter and set it aside. "I canna help but think Branwen will be glad for it. We had thought for so long that we wanted to experience the whirl of Edinburgh's social scene and quickly discovered it wasna as grand as we'd imagined."

He laid the letter aside and pointed to Bryston. "Bryston's next, I think."

She dutifully broke the seal and began reading. Halfway down the page, she gasped and shot Camden an astonished glance. "Sir Walter has been arrested for conspiracy."

"I suspected as much." Camden pulled his mouth into a grimace. "When Monteith was tipped off, I kent somethin' was fishy." He scratched his forehead. "Sir Walter had insisted we use the mercenaries in our missions, and somethin' never felt right about it."

She bit her lip as she finished reading the letter. "Bryston says Monteith was captured a week after he fled Edinburgh, and, to save his neck, blathered like a drunken tippler. He says yer letter about yer suspicions regarding Sir Walter helped him convince Monteith it would be in his best interest to talk."

Camden took it from her and gave a satisfied grunt. "I admit, I'm disappointed in Sir Walter. It just goes to show that men will do any sort of thing for money and power. He had me fooled until The Boar and Brew."

She leaned into him, nestling her head into the groove of his shoulder. "I'm sorry. I ken ye must be verra disappointed."

His chest expanded as he drew in a breath. The rhythmic beating of his heart beneath Bethea's ear brought her the oddest sense of peace.

"I canna say I'm no', but I'd already decided no' to continue as an agent, highwayman, or a marauder." He brought his other arm around to pull her flush to him and kissed her forehead. "I've accepted a much more excitin' and satisfyin' mission. Playin' husband to the most entrancin' woman in Scotland."

"Keep that up, and we'll never get to the king's missive," she murmured, blinking back tears of joy.

"His Majesty would be most offended to hear ye say it." He squeezed her waist. "Let's see what his royal pomposity has to say to me. I confess he's never deigned to write to me before."

Bethea dutifully collected the letter. A finger at the royal seal, she hesitated. "Shall I?"

"I told ye. Nae secrets. Open it, Bethea."

Undeniably curious, she cracked the seal and unfolded the expensive paper. "Och, Camden." She dropped the paper and threw herself into his arms, crying and laughing at the same time. "He's awarded ye and Bryston The Most Ancient and Most Noble Order of the Thistle. He has also bestowed estates on ye to thank ye for yer service in apprehending the leaders of the conspiracy against him."

Joyous tears blurred her vision.

"What?" He straightened, such an expression of complete astonishment on his face that she laughed. "I never expected anything of the sort."

Of course, he hadn't. He'd done what he did because he was an honorable man.

Nodding eagerly, she thrust the letter at him. "See for yerself. Ye're to appear at court as soon as 'tis convenient."

He read the letter, then, to her astonishment, tossed it onto the floor. "I have a much better award awaitin' me right here in this bed. A lass who loves me. Nothin' else will ever compare."

Opening his arms, he invited her into his embrace, and she went without hesitation.

"On second thought," he murmured, yanking the sheets down and positioning her legs to wrap around his waist, "I believe we'll explore a few more positions with me on the top, Wife."

"Och, that's a verra good idea, Husband."

EPILOGUE

Trentwick Castle
Scottish Highlands
8 August 1721

Holding a bouquet of heather, ivy, and roses, Bethea beamed as Keane walked Branwen down Trentwick Castle's small but beautiful chapel. Her sister had found love too.

She glanced at the tall, handsome man she'd called husband for the past four and a half months.

His loving gaze bathed her, as he no doubt remembered their unromantic, rushed ceremony in The Boar and Brew Inn. Beside Camden, Bryston couldn't tear his gaze off his bride, but neither had Branwen shifted her focus from her soon-to-be husband.

Elena and Cora, wearing matching purple gowns and carrying baskets of flower petals which they tossed before them, preceded Branwen. When they reached the end of the aisle, Marjorie beckoned them to sit with her, and giggling, they complied.

Bethea shifted slightly, taking in the assembled wedding guests. All of their closest friends were here, and her heart was full to overflowing.

Graeme and Berget Kennedy shared a pew with Liam and Emeline MacKay. Behind them, cousins Logan and Mayra Rutherford, and Coburn and Arieen Wallace smiled as they watched the bride's progression.

On the chapel's other side, Broden McGregor had his arm draped about Kendra's shoulders, and Quinn and Skye Catherwood shared a quick kiss.

Despite the odds, all of these couples had found true love in a time when marriages of convenience and arranged marriages were the norm.

Camden caught her eye again and mouthed, "I love ye." His gaze held a hot promise Bethea couldn't wait to explore. As impossible as it seemed, she grew to love him more every day.

As Branwen and Bryston exchanged their vows, Bethea's attention never left Camden. Their gazes remained entwined as if it were them reaffirming their commitment to each other.

Shortly, the jovial cleric was naming Branwen and Bryston husband and wife, and Bryston drew his bride into his arms.

Amidst well-wishes, Branwen and her new husband made their way down the aisle, and Bethea stepped to meet Camden. Her emotions high, she blinked back happy tears. "And here I worried Branwen and I would end up old tabbies."

He placed her arm in the crook of his elbow, and as always, a thrill of awareness coursed through her. When she was old and gray, she'd feel the same way about him. He was her other half.

"I'm sorry ye didna have a nice ceremony, Bethea." True chagrin shone in his eyes.

She smiled and shook her head. Her white and lavender gown rustled around her ankles as they stepped outside into a stunning Highland morning. "I'm nae sorry, Camden. Ye rescued me, and how many lasses can say they married their hero?"

A rueful smile tilted his mouth, and a mischievous gleam lit his blue eyes. "Well, there's Emeline, Berget, Arieen—"

She elbowed him in the side. "Ye ken what I mean."

"Aye, I do."

He glanced around at the guests congratulating the newlyweds as the crowd merged toward Trentwick for the wedding breakfast. Catching her hand in his, he hurried her around to the back of the chapel.

"What are ye doin?" she asked, hiking her gown up to keep from tripping. "We'll be missed, Camden."

Once out of sight, he gave her a wolfish grin and advanced upon her until her back was against the chapel's cool stones. They felt gloriously cool, as the day promised to be warm.

"Camden?"

When he met her gaze, his a sexy promise, lust coursed through her, turning her joints to jelly. *Lord*, he could undo her with his gaze.

"I promised ye I'd take ye against a wall, lass."

"Indeed, ye did."

And with the birds chirping, the grasses and leaves rustling in the summer breeze, and the fading voices of the wedding party and guests, Camden proved—very thoroughly—precisely how enjoyable a feat that was.

If you'd like to leave a review, please scan the QR code.

Keep reading for a free preview of
TO BARGAIN WITH A HIGHLAND BUCCANEER
Heart of a Scot Series, Book Eight

TO BARGAIN WITH A HIGHLAND BUCCANEER

©BLUE ROSE ROMANCE® LLC

12 April 1721
Holyrood Abbey
Leith, Scotland

Branwen Glanville couldn't prevent the slight shiver parading the length of her spine as she craned her neck, studying what was left of Holyrood Abbey's majestic chapel. Though sunny —the sky was a bright blue—the crisp air held an unmistakable chill.

Not at all uncommon for coastal Scotland—any part of Scotland, for that matter.

And yet, as accustomed as she was to Scotland's less than genial clime, another shudder rippled through her. Almost— *aye, almost*—as if in premonition of something sinister or ominous.

But what?

Holding her hood in place against the persistent, briny breeze tugging at the soft material, she glanced around the sun-drenched grounds. The golden rays shining through the remnants of the church's elaborate entrance cast striking shadows on the lush green lawns spread out below.

Nothing struck her as odd or drew her attention despite the overall atmosphere of melancholy and decades of awed reverence permeating the holy remains.

So why couldn't she shake this unwarranted sense of unease?

A dozen or so other people besides her family wandered the ruins as the mischievous breeze toyed with the long blades of verdant grass, plump, newly budded leaves, and the hem of her cloak with impartial precociousness.

Drawing her dark plum-colored velvet cloak tighter, she squinted at a rook watching her from atop an elaborately constructed arched stone wall. The light glinted off the bird's glossy plumage—an almost metallic blue hue colored its black wings. It dipped its head, rubbing its beak several times against the pale stone before flying off amid raucous squawks.

Probably to join its family or mayhap feed its young. In the distance, she watched as four other rooks joined the first. As they arched and spiraled their way through the sky, another three flew in loudly to meet them.

Unlike many people, she didn't believe crows, ravens, or rooks portended evil. In fact, she admired the species for their intelligence, cleverness, and dedication to their families.

Mayhap she was partial to them because her name meant blessed or fair raven, depending on which Welsh translation one preferred.

She squinted at the birds as they became smaller and smaller, eventually fading from sight in the distance. Although, now that she pondered on it, a gathering of crows *was* called a murder and a group of ravens a conspiracy.

Crows and ravens arena rooks, she chided herself.

Nae, but they are related.

Shaking her head once to dismiss her silly ruminations, Branwen returned her regard to the once glorious hallowed building.

Farther along the impressive bones of the abbey, Branwen's guardian, Keane Buchannan, the Duke of Roxdale, held his stepdaughter Cora's hand and his wife, Marjorie, held her other daughter Elana's hand as they inspected a pair of empty stone coffins.

Many decades before—perhaps centuries even—nameless marauders had desecrated the graves, possibly in search of a valuable bauble or two. Or perchance, the vaults had been plundered during the Reformation when one religious order believed itself superior to another.

That ideology hadn't changed much in the centuries since, truth be told.

It mattered naught why the burial places had been ransacked, but Branwen felt a peculiar sense of pity for the dead who hadn't been permitted a peaceful eternal slumber. Even as fascinated as she was with history, it didn't seem right to disturb the deceased simply out of curiosity.

Och, well.

She gave a little roll of her shoulder.

What was done was done.

She trailed her gaze over the well-maintained grounds once more. Though only a mere shadow of its former splendor, the abbey possessed an eerie beauty as well as an aura of sadness. The passage of time had been much kinder to the adjacent palace.

Giving herself another mental shake for her morose musings on such a lovely day, Branwen raised her face to the sun. Allowing her eyelids to lower, she inhaled the refreshing air. It held the tang of the sea but also the pungent scent of freshly cut grass and the faintest fragrance of fruit tree blossoms wafting from the palace gardens.

Though Edinburgh was scarcely two miles away, Leith's air was far cleaner. No dingy, soot-laden clouds lingered overhead, blanketing all and sundry in choking gray, in large part due to the persistent winds blowing inland from the Firth of Forth.

Girlish giggles carried to her on that same insistent wind, and she opened her eyes, sweeping her mouth upward.

Elana and Cora were thoroughly enjoying today's outing. Grinning, exposing the front tooth she'd lost but two days ago, Cora waved at Branwen as she skipped beside her new papa, pointing at one thing or another.

Keane nodded with an appropriate amount of interest and genuine affection.

Branwen waved back, smiling in return.

She adored Marjorie's daughters, and Marjorie too. She was the older sister that Branwen and her sister, Bethea, had never had. Sweet-tempered, patient, but with a will of iron, she'd made a brilliant duchess. But more importantly, she'd taken to Keane's wards with genuine caring and friendship.

Branwen and her sister adored her.

At the thought of Bethea, Branwen's chest tightened, and her breath caught as if someone had pulled her stays far too tight. Loneliness and no small amount of worry vied for supremacy in the tangled knots where her stomach ought to be.

At this very moment, her dear sister and her new husband, Camden Kennedy, were cloistered at Glen Tormallan Lodge —Keane's hunting lodge outside Culloden—hiding from spies that had meant them harm.

All because in March, Branwen had injured her feet during an unfortunate dance with a cloddish lord, and Bethea had tried to help her. Branwen had craved the excitement of Edinburgh's social life until that fateful night when her sister had been abducted after overhearing a plot to depose the king.

Thankfully, the spies had been apprehended, and Bethea and Camden were safe.

Now, however, Branwen found she far preferred the many historical sites in and around Edinburgh, as well as Leith's fascinating seaport, to social gatherings. And she missed the Highland's craggy beauty more than she'd imagined possible.

Stepping over a rock, which likely had fallen from the abbey's missing ceiling, Branwen mused to herself. She supposed as the daughter of a ship's captain, perhaps a bit of mariner's blood ran in her veins.

Until recently, she'd not thought a great deal about her father's livelihood. After all, she'd been a wee lass of five when her parents had been lost at sea during a tempest.

Raised at Trentwick Castle, high in the Scottish Highlands, she'd never realized how much the ocean appealed to her. But the sound of the waves greeting the shore, the briskness of the playful breeze, and the strident calls of the sea birds touched something deep within her.

Stirred something. Awoken a hunger Branwen hadn't known she possessed.

With a final glance at the abbey, she retraced her steps to the entrance and gazed in the direction of Leith's docks. As much as she'd enjoyed poking around the church's ruins, her real interest lay at the port, where the masts of ship after ship stood in the distance like faithful, nautical sentinels.

A yearning to board one of those vessels and sail into the sunset, headed for foreign lands, engulfed her. At the inexplicable longing, her breath and heart stalled for a heartbeat.

Such a wish was a fanciful dream. Keane held no interest

in ever leaving Scotland. Marjorie either, for that matter. She even abhorred travel by coach.

A small frown puckered Branwen's brow.

Her guardian and his wife were as content to remain in Scotland their entire lives as mice in a well-stocked larder.

Pursing her mouth, she hunched further into her heavy cloak, wishing she'd worn a heavier woolen gown and shawl.

She hadn't considered that after walking here, spending an hour or so poking around the ruins, and then walking into Leith before returning to Edinburgh, she might become chilled. That had been foolish of her, but she wasn't about to complain or express her discomfort.

Keane had agreed—after considerable cajoling—that they might stroll the docks and admire the many ships in port, accompanied by Keane's friend, Bryston McPherson. Bryston had recently returned from his mission in England. In point of fact, he'd been appointed to deliver one of the traitors responsible for Bethea's abduction to His Majesty's dungeons.

He was to meet them at eleven of the clock, the only reason Keane had agreed to Branwen's request to explore the abbey and wharf.

A seafaring man himself but also an agent for the crown, at six feet, four inches tall and comparable in size to an oak tree, Bryston would act as their unofficial bodyguard and tour guide.

Oh, Branwen wasn't fooled as to why Keane had asked Bryston to accompany them.

Scarred and tattooed, his Viking heritage on display for all to see, the Highland warrior fairly exuded power, strength, and intimidation. In truth, he'd frightened the stuffing out of her the first time she'd come upon him in the great hall eight years ago—before he'd acquired the scar that ran the length of his cheek now.

She'd been a gangly twelve-year-old in braids, and he a strapping nineteen-year-old, wilder than even the untamed Scots she'd become accustomed to. Then he'd winked and given her a crooked smile—an almost boyish grin—and her fear had dissipated as swiftly as fog upon a loch in the summer sun.

Bryston possessed stormy eyes—deterrents to unwanted conversation—a marble-like jaw, a mouth generally pulled into an unyielding, grim line, and a warrior's sculpted form, which made men and women tremble.

The former in fear and the latter in feminine awareness.

Not that she suffered from such womanly afflictions.

Good heavens, nae.

Truth be known, men of his ilk paraded in and out of Trentwick regularly. She was hardly the sort of woman to turn into a quivering custard at the site of a virile man's flexing muscles or a beard-stubbled jawline.

However, with Bryston and Keane in attendance as they visited the wharf, no one with a lick of common sense would cast so much as a gimlet eye in Branwen and Marjorie's direction today.

Naturally, even accompanied by two capable protectors, neither she nor Marjorie would be permitted to wander the unsavory lanes that always seemed to stretch out from dockyards like great depraved vines.

Still, Bryston had advised Keane that there was a charming tavern on Abbey Strand, which provided a partial view of the harbor, where they might partake in a midday meal before returning to Edinburgh this afternoon.

Branwen sighed as she reached the abbey's arched entrance and rested a shoulder against the nearly five-centuries-old structure. She wasn't sure what had plagued her of late, but a discontentment whirled through her at least once a day.

In general, it occurred when she permitted her mind to wander to her future and contemplated what her life would be like now that Bethea was married. Keane too. She felt as if she were an unnecessary fifth wheel. No one would ever hint at any such thing, but what newlyweds wanted another person underfoot constantly?

Only, she wasn't sure what it was she wanted. What, precisely, it was that she lacked or craved. Or why this new unrest seemed to expand daily. At Trentwick Castle, she'd believed it was because Keane had been so protective, rarely allowing her or Bethea to attend any functions.

He'd had his reasons, of course.

Good reasons, in truth.

His own mother had been set upon, ravished, and impregnated by a blackguard. Marjorie—bless the woman—had been instrumental in convincing him to relax his strictures and permit his wards this time in Edinburgh.

Undeniably, Branwen had enjoyed the balls, assemblies, and routs. Though, in all honesty, she'd found Edinburgh's High Society somewhat less than cordial. Downright feral at times, if she were perfectly candid.

As she scanned the horizon, a tall, solidly built man caught her attention, and a queer fluttering began behind her breastbone as if a half dozen blue tits were trapped there before throttling to her throat.

Bryston McPherson.

I hope you enjoyed this free preview of
TO BARGAIN WITH A HIGHLAND BUCCANEER
Heart of a Scot
Book Eight

. . .

FROM THE DESK OF COLLETTE CAMERON®

Thank you for reading TO MARRY A HIGHLAND MARAUDER, the seventh book in my HEART OF SCOT series.

For the authentic history buffs among you, I completely contrived the whole business about a conspiracy to overthrow King George I. While it's true he wasn't a popular king, and there were some minor Jacobite risings during his reign, everything I wrote regarding a list of Scots peers and lairds was pure fabrication.

The information about Easter and Wester Roads being the main passages into Edinburgh is true. It's also true there was a walking path called Leith Walk, which wasn't open to wheeled traffic until much later in the 17th century.

Unlike England, where divorces were almost impossible to acquire, divorces were somewhat easier to obtain in Scotland. As with any divorce, particularly for the woman involved, scandal always accompanied the dissolution of a marriage.

I hope you found a few hours of enjoyment with Camden and Bethea. If so, be sure to leave a review and check out the other books in my HEART OF A SCOT series.

To make sure you don't miss any of my book news, subscribe to my newsletter (Get a free book too!). I also have a fabulous VIP Reader Group on Facebook, Collette's Chéris. If you're a fan of my books and historical romance, I'd love to have you join me. You'll also be the first to see new covers, read exclusive excerpts, be the first to know about contests and give-aways, help me pick titles and name characters, and much, much more.

Please consider telling other readers why you enjoyed this book by reviewing it as well. I also truly adore hearing from my readers. You can contact me on my www.collettecameron-books.com and while you are there, explore my author world.

Hugs,
Collette

If you haven't joined Collette's exclusive mailing list click on QR image to sign up! You'll get access to exclusive content, sneak peeks, contests, giveaways, and more...
(P.S. No spam!)

https://collettecameronbooks.com/freegift

Collette loves to hear from readers.
You can contact her via her website: collettecameron-books.com.
Or email her directly at collette@collettecameron-books.com.

You can also follow Collette on social media:
Facebook: https://www.-facebook.com/ColletteCameronNovels/
Instagram: https://instagram.com/collettecameronauthor/
Goodreads: https://www.goodreads.com/collettecameron
Book Bub: https://www.bookbub.com/authors/collette-cameron

Pinterest: http://www.pinterest.com/colletteauthor/
YouTube: https://www.youtube.com/@ColletteCamero-nAuthor

Giggles are Guaranteed
Collette's Cheris Reader Group

https://www.facebook.com/groups/CollettesCheris/

If you love to chat about all things romance-book related and enjoy taking part in fun and engaging live events, contests, and giveaways join **Collette's Chèris VIP Reader Group, https://www.facebook.com/groups/CollettesCheris/,** my exclusive private book group on Facebook.

Giggles are guaranteed!

Hope to see you there,
Collette Cameron®

ABOUT THE AUTHOR

COLLETTE CAMERON®

USA Today Bestselling author Collette Cameron® is renowned for her captivating, humorous, and heartwarming Scottish and Regency historical romance novels. With over 65 published titles, over 1.6 million books sold around the world, and multiple writing awards to her credit, Collette is a well-known author in the world of historical romance.

Readers love her witty and relatable characters including daring rogues, dashing scoundrels, and the strong and spirited heroines who capture their hearts. From the rugged highlands to the refined drawing rooms of Regency England, Collette's novels will transport you to another time and place, where love and adventure are just a page away.

Collette's Sweet-to-Spicy Timeless Romances® are the perfect escape for readers looking for romantic escape, poignant inspiration, engaging humor, and entertaining stories.

Based in the Pacific Northwest, Collette is surrounded by the lush greenery and rainy skies that inspire her writing. She dreams of one day splitting her time between the Pacific Northwest and Scotland. In the meantime, she indulges in her love of all things cobalt blue, dachshunds, chocolate, and of course, crafting her next historical romance.

Blue Rose Romance® LLC
collette@collettecameronbooks.com
collettecameronbooks.com

~

FOR THE LOVE OF AN EARL (Wicked Earls' Club)

A Humorous Aristocrat and Wallflower

Regency Romance Adventure

~

HEART OF A SCOT

A Passionate Enemies to Lovers

Scottish Highlander Historical Mystery

Romance Adventure

HIGHLAND HEATHER ROMANCING A SCOT: CASTLE BRIDES

A Passionate Enemies to Lovers Second Chance Scottish Highlander Mystery Romance

~

LADIES OF OPPORTUNITY
A Bluestockings and Rogues Opposites Attract Regency Mystery Christmas Romance

The Wallflower's Wild Wager — Book 1

The Spinster's Secret Stake, Book 2

Better Not Bet a Bluestocking – Book 3

~

SECRETS OF SCANDALOUS LADIES
A Romantic Class Difference Forced Proximity Regency Romance with Aristocrats

A Lady's Scandalous Kiss — Book 1

No Lady for the Lord — Book 2

Love Lessons for a Lady — Book 3

His One and Only Lady — Book 4

Never a Proper Lady — Book 5

Lady Tempts a Rogue — Book 6

~

THE CULPEPPER MISSES
A Humorous Wallflower Family Saga Regency Romantic Comedy

The Earl and the Spinster — Book 1

The Marquis and the Vixen — Book 2

~

THE HONORABLE ROGUES®
A Second Chance Redeemable Rogue
and Wallflower Regency Romance